D0360083

BY AMANDA EYRE WARD

The Nearness of You

The
Nearness
of You

A Novel

AMANDA EYRE WARD

Ballantine Books
New York

Published in the United States by Ballantine Books, an imprint of Random House, a division of Penguin Random House LLC, New York.

BALLANTINE and the HOUSE colophon are registered trademarks of Penguin Random House LLC.

Library of Congress Cataloging-in-Publication Data

Names: Ward, Amanda Eyre, author.
Title: The nearness of you: a novel / Amanda Eyre Ward.
Description: First Edition. | New York: Ballantine Books [2017]
Identifiers: LCCN 2016034065 (print) | LCCN 2016039755 (ebook) | ISBN 9781101887158 (hardback) | ISBN 9781101887165 (ebook)
Subjects: LCSH: Domestic fiction. | BISAC: FICTION / Contemporary Women. | FICTION / Literary. | FICTION / Sagas.
Classification: LCC PS3623.A725 N43 2017 (print) | LCC PS3623.A725 (ebook) | DDC 813/.6—dc23 LC record available at https://lccn.loc.gov/2016034065

Printed in the United States of America on acid-free paper

randomhousebooks.com

987654321

First Edition

Book design by Diane Hobbing

For the mothers

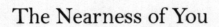

The Nearness of You

Prologue

The girl in the bed was close to death. There were no flowers on the bedside table, no balloons. It had been a pale day. A final strip of sun lit up the girl's motionless hands. Her fingernails were painted rose.

The nurse stood in the doorway, waited for the clock to reach five. Then she cleared her throat, and the three adults looked up. One was a man in his mid-fifties, wearing glasses and a cardigan sweater. A camel-hair coat hung over the chair behind him. The other adults were women. One was younger, with black hair pulled into a ponytail. She wore a parka, but had unzipped it to reveal a sweatshirt with a kitten decal. Her face was flushed, eyes red as if she had been crying, though she was not crying now.

The other woman was older but striking, with a dancer's posture and thick, red hair streaked with silver. She wore no makeup. Her face was luminous. She was not from around here.

"Visiting hours are over," said the nurse.

No one moved or spoke.

The nurse repeated, "Visiting hours are over." Still, the trio remained seated. "To clarify," said the nurse—if she'd said it once, she'd said it a million times—"only immediate family can stay past five P.M."

4 Amanda Eyre Ward

"I'm her father," said the man in a hoarse voice.

"OK," said the nurse. "And which of you is her mother?"

There was a thick quiet, broken only by the sound of the ventilator; the girl's slow but steady breath.

"Who is her mother?" repeated the nurse.

Part One

Suzette

2000

———

1

"I love you," said Hyland, in a tone suggesting that whatever was to follow would be terrible.

"I love you, too," said Suzette. It was one of her rare days off, and they were having brunch. Hyland had ordered mimosas, a bad sign. After fifteen years of marriage, day drinking generally led to a queasy afternoon nap followed by dry mouths, pizza for dinner, and the sense that they should be having more sex. Thirty-nine was a confusing age.

"Are we celebrating something?" said Suzette, when the waitress (a white girl whose nose was pierced through the septum with a cylindrical ring) placed their champagne glasses on the table.

Hyland sat back in his chair, lifted his drink. "We're celebrating our life," he said. "Life! We are celebrating life."

If he'd had some sort of terminal diagnosis, Suzette would know. Wouldn't she know? Surely, someone at the hospital would have told her. But there were many hospitals in Houston. "Are you . . . sick?" she ventured.

"Sick? No, no!" said Hyland. But his face was weird as he gazed at her. In fact, he was looking at Suzette as if *she* were ill, her demise imminent—a combination of adoration and teary gratitude.

Suzette was mad about her husband, but she hated this expression.

"Hyland," she said, pointedly sipping her ice water. "Something's going on. Just tell me."

"I'm sorry," said Hyland. He clasped her hands in a hot grip. "But it's not a surprise. It's a realization. OK? And will you hear me out?"

Suzette nodded warily. "Go on," she said.

"Do you want to order first?" said Hyland. "Yum, blueberry buckwheat pancakes!"

"Out with it, Hyland."

"OK. OK, honey. Here's what it is. I was jogging on Wednesday, you know, around the neighborhood. I was . . . Well, you know I've been unhappy at work."

Suzette nodded. Her stomach eased. He was going to quit his job. No matter: Hyland, who had thought he'd be an artist, had worked at six different architecture firms since getting his degree, his mood circling from elated to morose, then back again with each new office. Suzette made enough money. She wanted Hyland to be the optimistic man she had married—she depended on it—and if leaving Glencoe & Associates would return him to himself, she was all for it. She nodded sympathetically, picking up her mimosa.

"And I thought, I've been thinking, *Is this it?* I mean, we have our work, the house, the garden, but I mean—is that all?"

"Is this about your job?" said Suzette hopefully.

"No," said Hyland. "It's about— And please listen. It's about. Well, it's about a baby."

Fear shot through Suzette. She had a sudden urge to stand up and throw her drink across the room. But she gathered herself. She breathed in slowly (*Count to four,* she heard the British narrator of her "Meditation for Anxiety" cassette tape intone); she held her breath, then exhaled (*four, five, good work then . . . and six*). She cleared her throat. "No," said Suzette. "No, Hyland. Honey, please. We've decided. Haven't we decided?"

He held up his hand, nodding. "But what if we didn't have to use . . . what if it were my baby—but with a surrogate mother? Not even *one cell* of Crazy Carolyn. Just a baby that's biologically mine and otherwise both of ours. It's not so strange."

"You've thought about this," said Suzette, feeling hollow. She wanted to cry, but hadn't cried in twenty years. "Hyland, we agreed . . ."

He nodded. She'd told him she didn't want children on their first date. She'd said it simply, as soon as she realized how intriguing she found Hyland, and also how calm he was—and *kind*, a quality she'd almost given up on, especially amongst the overwrought medical school colleagues she'd been dating.

So many years ago: they'd finished their enchiladas and headed outside. Hyland couldn't wait to show Suzette his favorite museum, a few blocks away from La Tapatia Taqueria. "There's something I need to tell you," Suzette had said.

"Yes?" Hyland wore jeans and a Mexican wedding shirt with elaborate embroidery. Suzette had chosen one of her two sundresses for the blind date. Her closet was bare: she had no money and had lived for the past year in medical scrubs, even sleeping in them between shifts.

"My mom is very sick," said Suzette, pushing her hair behind her ears and looking past him, focusing on a live oak. "Mentally. She has a very bad mental illness. She's—she's in an institution now, and she will probably always be there."

Suzette saw that she had his full attention. His gaze was expectant but not surprised. Suzette exhaled. She was tired of telling this story, not embarrassed but simply *over it*. She hadn't talked to her mother in years. As far as she was concerned, Carolyn was dead.

"And I . . . I was sick, too, in college," Suzette continued. "Mentally. But I'm fine now. I take medication, and I guess there's always the risk that I'll . . ." She could scarcely speak—the memory of the year she'd suffered was too awful to summon: the black terror and desolation, the difficulty of living from minute to minute. When she'd been unable to bear the pain a moment longer, she'd swallowed a bottle of sleeping pills. Her college roommate had returned from a date early, and Suzette was finally put on the meds that saved her, and had kept her pretty much sane ever since.

"Anyway," Suzette continued, "I never want to have, um, children. I want this sickness . . . to end with me."

"Where?" said Hyland.

His question was so unexpected that Suzette laughed, stunned, then managed, "Where what?"

"Where's your mom?"

"Oh," said Suzette. "It's in New York. She's in New York. That's where I'm from."

"Me, too," said Hyland.

"You too what?" said Suzette. Her head was spinning.

"I'm from New York. Upper East Side. I grew up with my . . . with relatives on East Seventy-ninth."

Suzette nodded. Relatives? She decided not to ask, not yet. "My mom's at Bellevue."

It was a strange prelude to a first kiss. But Hyland leaned toward her and she closed her eyes. His lips on hers, his mouth. It was love, it really was love.

After the kiss, they continued walking to the Dan Flavin installation. Hyland (who still thought he'd be a famous artist himself) took Suzette's hand amongst the tubes of glowing neon, turning once in a while to absorb her bewildered-but-blissful expression.

"Do you get it?" he asked, in the main hall. Neon lights pulsed—

pink, yellow, green, blue—and Suzette stared down, where the concrete floor seemed a river of color.

"No," admitted Suzette. "But I love it."

"Then you get it," said Hyland.

They returned to his small rental house in Montrose, where he tried to make bananas Foster, setting off his fire alarm after igniting a pan of rum. By the time they figured out how to turn off the alarm and ate the dessert, it was evening. They drank cold beer on Hyland's front porch, then made love. When Suzette woke in the middle of the night, she felt a cool peace over her like water, her stomach calm. She looked at Hyland, touched his face, knew she'd do anything to keep him, to never return to the way she'd been just hours before: scared, dislocated, alone. They were married the following year by a justice of the peace, then took their four best friends to Goode Company Seafood for *campechana*, oyster po' boys, and champagne. (They'd had to live on beans and rice for a month to save up for the celebration, and it was worth every penny.)

Now, he sighed. "You're right," he said. "I know. We did agree." And there was so much sadness in the words that Suzette was taken aback. Hyland looked at her. His parents and sister had been killed in a car accident when he was eleven. He'd told her, in their early courtship, that he'd always dreamed of having children, of seeing his mother's face in them. He'd broken off their engagement over it, said it was just too important to him. But then, in the most wonderful turn of events, he'd changed his mind, and they were happy.

"I thought we were happy," said Suzette.

But Hyland did not reply.

That night, Suzette lay awake, despite the Ambien. She tried deep breathing, then the meditation tape on her Walkman—the man with a British accent told her to "just check in" with each of her organs: *How do your lungs feel today? Good? Tired? No need to change anything, just take note. And your colon? How does your colon feel?*

Suzette pulled off her headphones. She had a full day ahead at the hospital and needed to sleep. But no matter which way she arranged herself, Suzette could not let go. A baby. What if it were possible to have a baby? Because of her brain and her mother's brain (and God knew, probably her grandparents' brains before that), Suzette had never allowed herself to yearn for a child.

A baby, warm on her chest. A toddler and a bag of breadcrumbs to feed the ducks in the park. The chance to erase her past, to begin anew. Suzette discovered that she liked the idea of the child being Hyland's, a zygote formed with his sperm and the egg of someone young and sweet, someone who would disappear from the picture after a safe and joyous birth. (Bonus: Suzette would not have to give birth! Labor—its utter unpredictability, the brute nature of the act—had always terrified her. She was a surgeon for a reason, and that reason was complete control.)

As the pill lowered its leaden curtain, zonking Suzette's mind into silence, she curled up, lay on her side. *Oh, maybe,* she thought: a warm girl, the nape of her neck smelling of baby shampoo . . .

2

It was a lark for Suzette, at first. Nerve-racking, yes, but exciting. There were piles of folders—so many young eggs! So many wombs for rent! The best chance for conception was traditional surrogacy: Hyland would medically impregnate someone young(er), who would carry the baby to term. Suzette could keep working without interruption and Hyland would sire a child. It was a win-win all around.

Late at night, though, Suzette panicked. It seemed straightforward, clinical, but something deep within her was disturbed. She thought of backing out, but Hyland was so damn *thrilled*—she hadn't seen him like this in . . . well, ever. And she felt a fragile hope herself. A child—Hyland's child—had been more than she'd ever dared to want. And yet, why not?

Because she was scared. Suzette still felt surprised by her good luck each night when she came home and Hyland was not only still there but still loved her. It was some sort of post-traumatic stress thing, she assumed: due to her miserable childhood, Suzette's fight-or-flight response was all out of whack and she saw normal life as precarious. She tried to tamp down her terror, sat next to her husband as he paged through the donor profiles. He kept his hand on her knee, knowing her, knowing she was like a spooked animal.

In the middle of May, they chose a donor named Gail. Gail looked quite a bit like Suzette, actually: red hair and green eyes. But she was twenty-nine years old and had already given birth to two biological children and two surrogate babies, one for a gay couple in Arlington and one for a straight couple in Port Aransas. She kept a diary on her MySpace page, and Suzette spent her lunch break poring over it, reading about each of Gail's pregnancies (a craving for peanut butter was a recurring theme) and staring at pictures of Gail's children. Gail also had a husband, Oliver, who posed cheerily next to his constantly pregnant wife at bowling alleys and on a fishing boat.

Gail lived in Sugar Land, a Houston suburb that had been built atop a sugar plantation. Gail wrote that Oliver worked "in the construction arena." Suzette surmised that the $35,000 each surrogate birth brought in helped pay for the boat and matching trucks (with vanity plates reading HIZ and HERZ).

"I don't know," said Pam, the head nurse, looking over Suzette's shoulder at her computer screen.

"She's cute, though, don't you think?" said Suzette.

"Sure," said Pam. "But Dodge Rams? You drive a Lexus."

"What's your point?" said Suzette irritably.

"You're classy," said Pam. "That's all I'm saying."

Despite herself, Suzette was flattered. "Get scrubbed in," she said.

"Yes, boss," said Pam.

But before Suzette had time to prep for her 1:00 P.M. angiogram, she was paged for a donor run. An ambulance waited outside St. Luke's, and Suzette called Hyland as it sped her through the city to the airport. "I don't know how long I'll be," she said.

"We're supposed to meet Gail and Oliver," said Hyland. "At Applebee's."

"I know," said Suzette. "I'm sorry."

"OK," said Hyland.

"Honey," said Suzette.

"I know," said Hyland. "You don't have to say it."

The ambulance turned in to George Bush Intercontinental Airport, following signs to John F. Kennedy Boulevard. Suzette peered out the window as they drove onto the tarmac, parking next to a private jet. "We're here," said Suzette. "At the jet. I have to go."

"Goodbye," said Hyland, cutting the line.

Suzette sighed, closed the phone, and stepped out of the ambulance. She nodded to the pilot, grabbed the transport cooler, and climbed the stairs to the passenger entrance of the jet.

"Six-week-old baby in Amarillo. Dallas didn't have a match," said Stefan Vaughn, the senior resident, who was already on the plane, flipping through the chart. "Motor vehicle accident. No insult to the heart. They did the second brain death exam an hour ago. Donor echo looks good."

Suzette nodded. They both acknowledged the baby's death with silence. The stewardess offered a basket of cheese and crackers. Suzette shook her head. She closed her eyes as the jet began to pick up speed, barreling down the runway. When they were airborne, she opened her eyes again. Stefan was spreading Brie on a Ritz cracker. "Come to think of it," said Suzette, "I will have a snack. And a coffee, please."

"Of course," said the stewardess, unbuckling her seatbelt and heading to the galley kitchen.

"I could get used to this," said Suzette.

Stefan nodded, brushing crumbs from his lips.

A waiting ambulance at Amarillo International Airport transported them to the hospital. The operating room was filled with teams of surgeons: the baby would give up both her lungs, eyes, and kidneys as well as her pancreas, liver, small intestine, skin, and bones. But everyone was waiting for Stefan and Suzette, as the heart was removed first, transforming the patient from a state of brain death to a body without a pulse. The tiny cadaver was already prepped and draped on the operating table, and Suzette was relieved—it broke her to see a dead baby in his or her entirety, though she never let on.

Suzette bowed her head. She tried to take a fraction of a second to be thankful for all the lives this sweet little girl would save. And then she got to work. Although quiet days seemed to hold menace for Suzette, when the risks were real she was utterly calm—in her element. She opened the baby's chest, clamped the aorta, cooled and removed the heart. It was no bigger than a rubber ball. Suzette placed the tiny organ in her palm.

"Nice, nice," said Stefan.

Suzette carried the heart to the transport cooler. "Let's go," she said.

Suzette and Stefan ran back to the ambulance. In Houston, a baby was being prepped for the donor heart, which would survive out of a body for only four hours, maybe less. When they landed, Suzette carried the cooler from the jet into another ambulance, which sped her back to St. Luke's.

Pam was waiting in the OR next to another tiny baby, this one pink—alive. Suzette glanced at the chart: a girl named Bella, three days old. Suzette put on her headlight, magnifying loupes, surgical cap, and mask. For seven agonizing minutes, she scrubbed her wrists, forearms, and hands. She slipped on her gloves. The circulating nurse tied her robe, and Suzette entered the OR. "What are you doing here?" she said to Pam.

"Double shift," said Pam.

Suzette inhaled, readying herself to transform a tragedy in Amarillo into a Houston miracle. To give life after ending life. The small, cool heart. The pulse of the oximeter. Her own hands—sterile, steady, unerring. Suzette loved her job fiercely. She reached for the scalpel.

When the operation was over, she took a shower and headed home. It was late, and she figured Hyland would be asleep. Suzette parked in their three-car garage next to Hyland's Volvo and took a moment—in the hushed dimness, her car engine ticking as it cooled—to feel proud.

In the kitchen, lined with wide windowsills on which Hyland grew herbs in deep blue pots, Suzette made a cup of tea, using the microwave instead of the expensive Italian teakettle perched on the six-burner stove. As Suzette waited for her water to boil, she looked at the Viking, which had been chosen by Hyland during the renovations she'd had little to do with. How did it turn on? She wasn't sure. On top of two burners was a giant slab of metal. A griddle? Who knew?

As a girl in upstate New York, Suzette had taught herself how to open a can with a knife. She took great pleasure in the fancy tea she could now afford—dried "Egyptian Chamomile blossoms" and "sweetly subtle citrus slices" enclosed in a "specially created silky Tea Pouch." In the low glow from the skylight that stretched across the kitchen ceiling, Suzette read the box: "Surrender and treat your palate to a sumptuous delight." Suzette breathed in the lavender scent of the cleaning products Nancy used to oil the floors and polish the appliances and counters each day, even when no one had cooked a thing. Nancy shopped, too, following Suzette and Hyland's lists to the letter. (She was better at choosing clothes for Suzette than Suzette was herself—the one-shouldered gown Suzette had worn to the Menil Collection Gala had been perfect.)

Hyland was not asleep. He was at his drafting table sipping

sake. Since a work trip to Kyoto the year before, he'd begun drinking sake in the evenings from a tiny ceramic cup. He was partial to the milky-looking Dreamy Clouds, which was difficult to find in the United States, but not impossible.

"How'd it go?" he said, looking up. Hyland wore pajama pants and a navy T-shirt, his feet bare on the rungs of his stool. He was heavier than he'd once been, but Suzette found his bulk attractive. Substantial. He looked important, with his pages of blueprints and mechanical pencil. Suzette loved his architect handwriting— the neat capital letters. She wondered if the maybe-baby would have his toes: long and thin, with oval toenails.

"Good," said Suzette.

"Well, it didn't go so well with Gail," said Hyland, turning to face her, his tone flat.

"Oh."

"She wants a mother who's involved," said Hyland.

Suzette felt as if she'd been slapped. "Did you explain the situation?" she said, her voice sharp.

"I'm just telling you what she said," said Hyland, opening his hands.

"That's not fair," said Suzette. She stood in the doorway, clutching her teacup.

"No, it isn't," said Hyland. His shoulders fell forward. "But it's a fact," he said. He rose from his desk and went into the living room, collapsing onto the low-slung leather sectional.

Suzette felt hot. She followed Hyland, sat down in the chair facing him. She set her cup on the glass table. "Well, to hell with her," she said.

Hyland shook his head, picked up *Artforum*, and pretended to read.

"We'll find someone else," said Suzette.

"I know," said Hyland. He put down the magazine and sighed.

"What is it?" said Suzette, reaching to touch his neck.

"I don't know," he said. Suzette moved next to him on the couch, put her arms around him. Her shaggy-haired Hyland. He put his head on her shoulder and she held him.

"I'm not going to apologize for doing my job," said Suzette, after a time. "You have to know that. I'm not going to stop being my best because of this . . ." She struggled for the words to define what they were doing, then repeated, "because of this."

He nodded, gathering himself, moving to the opposite side of the couch. They lay facing each other, legs outstretched and aligned. "I understand," he said. "I do."

"Then what's the matter?" said Suzette. He shook his head. Suzette lay back into the pillows. "Go on, say it," she said, grabbing his foot.

"Sometimes I have this dream," said Hyland. "We're married, and we live here in this same house. But every time you touch me, I can't talk. I'm mute or something. Like, I can open my mouth, but no sound comes out."

Suzette crossed her arms over her chest. "What is that supposed to mean?"

Hyland shrugged. "I'm not a dream analyst," he said. "I'm an architect."

"You should quit your job," said Suzette, picking up her teacup, taking a sip, then resting it on her stomach.

"You're probably right," said Hyland. "The Willie Nelson Condominiums are ruining my life. The splash pad. The mirrored walls. My God, I hate condo developments for young people."

"You could be a stay-at-home dad," said Suzette. "I could see it. Really, I could. You could hang out at the park, teach the baby to paint . . . make peanut butter and bacon sandwiches with the crusts cut off . . ."

"Now I'm hungry," said Hyland.

"Me, too," said Suzette.

"We actually have peanut butter *and* bacon," said Hyland, standing up and moving toward the kitchen.

"Oh my God, I love you," said Suzette. "Though I have to note that bacon is not fabulous for the arteries."

"No you don't," called Hyland, approaching the refrigerator.

Suzette laughed, following him. "I'll never get to see the truck called HIZ," she said.

"Nor HERZ," said Hyland, placing a cast-iron pan on the stove.

Suzette moved behind him, reached around his waist, and rested her head on her husband's strong back.

The bacon smelled delicious.

3

Months passed: the ordinary river of days, but one now shimmering with the possibility of something—of some*one*—more. After several failed connections, a self-described "devoted housewife" from West, Texas (not to be confused with West Texas), chose the Kendalls. Nina Cortez was thirty-two, her dossier filled with snapshots of her three biological children. This would be her first surrogacy. Nina was nervous, she told the Kendalls over a strip mall Chinese lunch.

"What do you mean *nervous?*" asked Hyland.

"So many things can go wrong," mused Nina.

"That's true," said Suzette, spooning wonton soup from a Styrofoam bowl.

"But so many things can also go right," said Hyland.

"I guess so," said Nina. "I mean, of course! Of course, Mr. Kendall."

"Call me Hyland, please."

Nina nodded, her smile forced. She began injecting herself with hormones that Friday, as soon as the check cleared.

• • •

A few weeks later, Hyland deposited his sperm into a sterile cup and returned to the fertility clinic waiting room. "All set?" said Suzette, putting down a two-year-old issue of *Good Housekeeping*.

Hyland nodded, blushing. He glanced around, but they didn't know any of the other couples. Suzette surmised they were a decade older than most. Hyland put his hands in the pockets of his khakis and rocked back on his sneakers. "Well . . ." he said.

Nina smiled at Suzette and Hyland, gathered her mint-colored handbag, and followed the nurse into Dr. Richmond's office. "Here goes!" she said, giving the Kendalls a thumbs-up.

Both Suzette and Hyland returned the gesture. When Nina was out of earshot, Hyland murmured, "Jesus, this is strange."

"Are we supposed to wait here?"

Hyland shrugged. "I guess so."

"Did they have, like, dirty magazines back there?" whispered Suzette.

"Do you really want to know?"

Suzette hesitated, then said, "Yes. I really do want to know."

"An old copy of *Hustler*."

"An old copy of *Hustler*," said Suzette thoughtfully.

"Yup," said Hyland.

Suzette felt uneasy. She took Hyland's hand and squeezed it.

"Well," said Hyland, "it's not like I'd imagined."

"I'm sorry," said Suzette. She gritted her teeth. She *was* sorry, deeply sorry that she couldn't be the easy, breezy, fertile wife Hyland might have wanted, but she was also weary of being made to feel that she was lacking. It was Hyland, after all, who'd changed the rules, who all of a sudden wasn't satisfied with all they had.

"You don't have to apologize," said Hyland.

"Right," said Suzette. She checked her beeper, but no one had paged her. She scrolled through old messages on her PalmPilot. There was the one from the clinic about Patricia, who had decided Hyland and Suzette were too old. There was the one about Harriett, who wanted to help a couple with "stronger faith." There were also replies from nanny services and a Baby Proof Expert named Lynn. And there was another note from her best friend, Meg, who wanted to see her, who missed her.

"I've got to call Meg," said Suzette.

"Now?" said Hyland.

Suzette understood that he wanted to hold these moments sacred—the moments of conception, though they were spent in a lemon-scented waiting room rather than their marital bed. Suzette had the fleeting thought that she should seduce him in the clinic restroom, but it seemed like a ton of effort, and he was likely spent from his laboratory orgasm. "Being parents isn't about this," she said. "It doesn't matter how we get her, or him. What matters comes later."

"I guess so," said Hyland.

Nina came out shortly afterward. She seemed surprised to see them. "Everything good?" said Hyland.

"Yes," said Nina. "All good. I'll call you when we find out if it . . . takes," she said.

"Sounds great!" said Hyland heartily.

"Thank you, Nina," said Suzette.

They drove home in silence, Suzette gazing out the passenger window at the trees, lush and verdant after a rainy spring. Houston was a city with personality—loud and bright, faintly marshy and rotten around the edges. Perhaps this was a place where she could be a mother. Suzette tried to imagine herself wearing a pink visor and a ponytail, driving a giant Voyager van. The image would not coalesce.

On the flagstone porch of their house, Suzette saw a trio of giant cardboard boxes. "What on earth?" she said.

"Oh, it's my stuff from New York," said Hyland.

"Your stuff from New York?" Suzette narrowed her eyes. She had no idea what he was talking about, and she didn't like it one bit.

"Some of the things from my . . . from my parents' house. It's all been in storage, all these years."

"Oh," said Suzette. She could not think of one thing else to say. Bitter panic rose in her chest.

"I thought maybe it was time," said Hyland.

Suzette had always seen his past as a clean slate: miserable, lonely, over with and done. She felt the same about her life before she'd met him. As a duo, they'd walked away from the burning houses of their youths and built anew. (Not literally—their home was built in the late sixties—but *metaphorically* they'd built a brand-new dwelling. Of dreams. Of hoping that everything would be OK and savoring the simple joys. But now, here were boxes of smoking embers, sitting on their porch, just waiting to ruin everything, to set fire to their . . . to their new . . . to their house built of hope . . .)

Suzette blinked, trying to ignore the incoherent chatter in her brain. She helped Hyland drag the boxes inside and watched as he opened them carefully with an X-Acto knife and removed framed photographs, baby blankets, boxes of papers. "There's furniture, too," said Hyland. "A whole house full."

Suzette made tea. Why had she never wondered what had happened to his dead family's belongings? Was this what a male midlife crisis looked like—a man close to tears, fondling his own baby blankets?

"It felt like it was time," Hyland repeated.

"OK," said Suzette. What did he mean by this? That a baby would want to see his or her grandparents' junk? Or that the thought of having a child had made Hyland nostalgic? Why had it not felt like the right time for the last fifteen years? Suzette told herself not to read too much into the boxes. They were just objects, after all. They weren't necessarily harbingers of doom. Although they certainly could be harbingers of doom.

Suzette picked up a photograph of a woman in a wedding gown. The woman had Hyland's heavy eyelids, his fine nose. Even her bemused expression was familiar. "Your mother," said Suzette with wonder.

Hyland nodded.

"She looks just like you."

"Yes."

"I never knew all this . . . existed."

"Yeah," said Hyland. "Aunt Deb told me everything was in storage. I called her last week, and she told me where."

"Last week?"

Hyland nodded, unfolding a child's sweater, releasing the scent of mothballs.

"Where should we put it all?" asked Suzette.

"The baby's room?" said Hyland. He had decided, without Suzette's input, that the upstairs office would become the "baby's room." All of Suzette's papers and the bills had been moved downstairs, and the desk set (not valuable, but one Suzette liked nonetheless) had been left by the curb for "large garbage" day.

"The baby's room," said Suzette miserably. "OK." One by one, they unpacked the objects. Suzette put the picture of Hyland's mother on the mantel. She put the blankets and clothing in the empty room. They were solemn as they handled the remains of Hyland's life before the accident.

"It can happen in an instant," said Hyland. Suzette thought of Nina Cortez, her womb, Hyland's baby.

"What if you love the baby more than me?" she said softly. "What if you leave me?"

"What did you say?" called Hyland, halfway up the stairs with a cardboard box.

She didn't answer. Four weeks later, when Nina called and said, "It didn't take," Suzette did not feel disappointed, but relieved.

4

Suzette was on call, but there wasn't any reason she couldn't get a pedicure at Perfection Nails from Lenny, the most attractive pedicurist in Houston. Meg texted that she was absolutely in, and the two met at the minimart attached to Perfection Nails, where Suzette grabbed a Twix bar and Meg a bottle of sauvignon blanc. "Don't judge," said Meg, pulling a coffee mug and wine opener from her purse.

"I would never," said Suzette. Though she was mercilessly critical of herself, Suzette had a live-and-let-live philosophy, shared with Hyland, that helped them maintain their wide circle of friends. The previous weekend, for example, they'd watched lawn tennis at the River Oaks Country Club with Suzette's chief resident and his charming socialite wife, followed by the opening party for a friend of Hyland's who had spent two years lurking around the Bronx, photographing young addicts underneath bridges and in dimly lit shooting galleries. On the way home from the exhibition, where cheap wine and pretzels had been served, they stopped in to have a late dinner with Hyland's sake supplier, Hiro, and Ralph, the musicology graduate student for whom Hiro had recently left his Japanese wife.

Perfection Nails was packed, as always. Everyone from sorority girls to trophy wives flocked to the strip mall salon off West-heimer to have their feet massaged by Lenny and his colleagues. Sure, Perfection Nails charged twice as much as every other salon, but each pedicure included a twenty-minute foot rub. As Meg said once, after Lenny had run his thumbs along her insoles, "Oh my sweet Lord. It's better than sex."

Meg had three children, whose car seats lined the jump seat of her pickup truck. She silk-screened T-shirts with Audubonish images of her own design, selling them every weekend at the farmers' market. She and Suzette had known each other since meeting at a matinee of Antonioni's *The Passenger* a decade be-fore. They were the only two in the theater: Meg was very preg-nant and bored, and Suzette was taking a rare afternoon to herself in the midst of her general surgery residency.

"I love Jack Nicholson," Meg had whispered, and Suzette had nodded her agreement.

"I love Junior Mints," Suzette had said, passing the open box.

"I love you for sharing your Junior Mints," Meg had said.

Now, Meg settled her feet into a hot, bubbling whirlpool and said, "OK, give me the update. Is anyone pregnant with your hus-band's sperm?"

"Nope, not yet," said Suzette. She opened her candy bar, then fiddled with the massage chair settings, leaning back into the ro-botic kneading. "Can I be honest?" she said.

"Suzette, pick a color," said Lenny.

"Oh, you choose," said Suzette. "Something happy." Her chair began to buzz and shake. "Um, Lenny?" she said. He stood up, wrested the control pad from her fingers, and switched the mas-sage to a gentler setting.

"Don't mess with it," said Lenny. He ran his fingers through his expertly styled hair, looking over the row of polishes. "I think cinnamon," he decided.

"Perfect," said Suzette.

"You can be honest," said Meg. "It's me."

Suzette smiled. She felt lucky, after a childhood of secrets, to have a friend who was with her no matter what. Meg had held her the first time Suzette had lost a patient. Meg had made her truffled popcorn and a martini when Suzette had arrived at her house after she and Hyland had fought viciously about his emails with an old flame. On Suzette's birthday every year, a day marked not just by time passing but by memories of her mother, Meg always took her out to a simple, comforting lunch and gave her flowers. She told Suzette how much she treasured their friendship—how much it meant to Meg to have a friend who saw her as *herself*, and not the harried mom she acted like 95 percent of the time. Suzette took a deep breath. "I'm not sure I want this. I'm just not sure about the baby. There, I've said it."

"You do want cinnamon or you don't want cinnamon?" said Lenny.

"Yes, Lenny, cinnamon," said Suzette. "Thank you."

"That's perfectly normal," said Meg, sipping wine from her coffee mug. She wore one of her own silk-screened T-shirts, jeans, and pink eyeglasses. "I didn't want any of my kids. I still don't."

"Meg!"

"Seriously. They make my entire life worthwhile—they are literally my whole reason for being, and I love each one so much my heart could burst—and yet I wish I didn't have them almost every day. Usually around six. When I'd really, really like to watch TV or make love . . . or take a nap . . . but instead, I have to give bubble baths and help with *math* homework and read books aloud that I have utterly no interest in."

Lenny caught Suzette's gaze and widened his eyes, smirking.

"What, Lenny?" said Meg. "Do you have kids?"

Lenny chuckled, saying, "No, no, no. No kids."

"Smart man," said Meg. Her toes were being handled by Bryce, also ridiculously attractive.

Suzette looked around the room, which was unremarkable but for the radiance on the faces of a dozen women. "So what are you saying—just go on and do it, even if you're scared to death?" she said. "Even if you already have a good life?"

"Yup, that's what I'm saying," said Meg. "Be brave. You're going to be fine." She reached for a *People* magazine.

"You're crazy," said Lenny, shaking his head. "Who needs children?"

"You don't want kids, Lenny?" said Meg. "Never ever?"

"No, never ever," said Lenny, who told Suzette every time she visited about his latest vacation: Aspen, Las Vegas, Orlando. "I'm all set already," said Lenny. "Why mess around?"

"Why mess around?" said Meg, nodding. She refilled her mug from the bottle on her tray table. "The man has a point," she said.

"Nina Cortez backed out," said Suzette. "But we've been matched with someone new. She's really young. A beautiful brunette. She works at Sea-O-Rama."

"The water park on Galveston?"

"The very one."

Meg took this in. "What does she do there?" she asked.

"She's an Animal Trainer in Training," said Suzette. "I believe she works specifically with penguins. And Hyland has his heart set on her. He says she's the one, he can tell. We're going to meet her this weekend."

Meg contemplated these facts in silence. She took a sip of her wine. "I don't like it," she said.

"Why not?"

"I just . . ." said Meg. "She sounds worrisome. Gorgeous, really? Can't you hire just a normal girl, just a mediocre one?"

"The whole thing . . ." said Suzette, shaking her head.

"Yeah, I hear you," said Meg.

"On the other hand, it could be wonderful."

"It could," said Meg. "It probably will be. I'm sorry this is so confusing."

"You need to know your own worth," said Lenny, who tended to make broad, inspiring proclamations. "Don't be the change. Be the dollar."

"I don't understand," said Suzette.

"Yes, Suzette, you do understand," said Lenny. "Be the dollar." And then he began to run his fingers around Suzette's ankles, and she stopped talking, stopped thinking, and closed her eyes.

"I am the dollar," she told herself.

5

And yet, and yet.

On the day of baby Bella's discharge, Suzette stood at the doorway, watching Bella's parents wrap her in a pink blanket, settling her into a brand-new baby car seat. "Hello," she said, "I'm Dr. Kendall. I just wanted to introduce myself and give Bella my best wishes."

"Oh," said Bella's mother, a slight woman in a long sundress. "I'm so glad we got to meet you. I'm so— Thank you. Thank you so much."

Bella's father strode forward. He was very young, clad in a KENT SCHOOL T-shirt, pleated shorts, and water sandals. He clasped Suzette's hand and pumped it forcefully. "You saved our baby," he said. "You fixed her, you gave her a good heart."

"It wasn't me," said Suzette, thinking of the baby in Amarillo, who had only had a few weeks in the world.

"Would you like to hold her?" asked Bella's mother.

Suzette shook her head, but Bella's mother moved toward her, holding out the baby. Suzette put her hand on Bella's chest, feeling the donor heart beating. Bella's blue eyes were open. Suzette accepted the baby, held her to her own rib cage. She smelled the baby's skin, and felt her wriggling, hot body.

I want this, thought Suzette. *OK, yes. I want this.*

Could Suzette be a mother, and a dollar?

6

The first and only time the Kendalls had been to Galveston Island, located an hour and a half from Houston, had been to visit the condominium of their friends the Schroeders at a development called Dancing Dunes, which had since gone belly-up. It had been a nice enough resort, intentionally reminiscent of Cape Cod, with white clapboard houses and rickety boardwalks leading to the beach. The developers had even gone so far as to name the streets after Massachusetts locales: P-Town Way, Woods Hole Avenue, Cataumet Lane, Falmouth Road, and (jarringly) Southie Circle.

But the only place to have dinner was Martha's Rockin' Vineyard, a combination snack bar/disco that was so loud and rowdy—filled with tattooed, sunburned Texans—that even Suzette, who hadn't cooked since she was eighteen, had agreed to help make dinner at the condo, chopping peppers into dissimilar shapes with great consternation.

"Remember that night you had too much beer and got lost on the way back to the Schroeders'?" said Suzette now, as Hyland piloted the Volvo onto I-10 out of Houston.

"I do," said Hyland. "And you guys had so many margaritas you forgot I wasn't there and locked the condo, and when I finally found you, I couldn't get in, and I had to sleep in the bed of Carl's truck? And then it rained? On Buzzards Bay Way?"

"Yeesh," said Suzette. "We were kind of a mess." Hyland shook his head. Carl Schroeder was now the city controller.

Hyland turned on the radio, flipping until he found classical music. "Calming," he noted.

"Remember when we smoked cigarettes?" said Suzette.

"American Spirits. That was a fun summer," said Hyland.

"And the cans of rum-and-Coke in Costa Rica?"

"You can still have rum," said Hyland. "That's one of the perks of surrogacy."

Suzette's laugh was dry, a bit bewildered. Suddenly the whole endeavor—meeting a strange girl on Galveston Island, offering to pay her to be a surrogate mother due to Suzette's inability to move on from her childhood, despite all assurances that her life with Hyland was secure, loving, and peaceful—the whole endeavor seemed sordid. What if she just put her fears aside and tried to get pregnant on her own? No sooner had the thought entered her mind than she saw her mother's face, illuminated by firelight, on one of those nights when she wouldn't use electricity, because the government could come through the wires. "No way," said Suzette.

"What?"

She sighed. "This is hard," she said. "It's just hard."

Hyland turned up the radio: Liszt. They listened to the rainstorm of notes. Suzette tried to summon the British man and his guided meditation. *Just check in. How does your stomach feel? Don't try to change it, just take note.*

My stomach feels crappy, thought Suzette.

They drove. The land flattened and the gulf came into view. Suzette gazed at Texas City to her left, the bizarre pyramids of Moody Gardens to her right. It had been easier to ignore what humans did to the planet during her childhood in upstate New

York, where it was clear that Mother Nature was in charge. Here, human folly was on proud display: the refineries sending up plumes of toxic smoke, the water that left a tarry residue on your skin, the pier covered with amusement park rides for those who weren't duly amused by the sea.

The Yo Ho Ho restaurant was flanked by an enormous fac-simile of a shark's head—people could stand inside the mouth and pretend they were being eaten. "I've got my camera," said Hyland playfully.

"Oh my God, no," said Suzette. She smoothed her pants.

"Do not use the Lord's name in vain," said Hyland. Suzette snorted. The clinic had told them that Dorothy was religious. Both she and her mother worked at Sea-O-Rama. Dorothy was a high school graduate and planned to use the Kendalls' money to go to college. The clinic generally advised against single women, and also against women who had not had previous children.

"So if you *advise against* this person, why did you send us her file?" said Suzette, exasperated.

"Your choice of surrogate is ultimately your choice," said the clinic secretary, Margaret.

Suzette sighed. "Are there legal problems or what?" she said.

Margaret spoke slowly, obviously arranging her words with care. "Dr. Kendall, the laws regarding surrogacy are various and vary from state to state. In Texas, you are completely protected no matter what the marital status of your surrogate ends up to be, as long as she signs the Fertility Clinic of Houston documents. In my experience, all different walks of life can provide a wonderful surrogate experience."

"Thank you, Margaret," said Suzette, snapping shut her phone.

So there were risks. This was nothing they didn't already know. But when Suzette looked back on it later, when she tried to remember who she and Hyland had been—two kids, really—overgrown kids, but innocent, holding hands and entering the

Yo Ho Ho, smiling at each other, so full of excitement—she had to admit that they were desperate. Did they ignore the signs?

Look at them: Hyland in his seersucker pants and button-down shirt, his too-long hair, his eyes bright with hope. Suzette, wary but willing to be convinced. They are still clasping hands as the hostess, a girl in a pirate costume, leads them to a leather banquette. They sit next to each other nervously. And in she walks: a radiant young girl with curly black hair and an open face. They rise. She walks toward them. It is all there from the very start—she is fertile, unstable, beautiful.

"Hello," the girl says. "My name is Dorrie."

7

Suzette was already scrubbed in when Leslie appeared at the door of the operating room, her palms spread wide in distress. "Sorry, I'm sorry!" she cried. While Leslie kept a level head during even the most dire medical emergencies, she tended to lose her cool over innocuous concerns: unidentified coffee mugs, who was supposed to be whose Secret Santa, vanilla versus chocolate sheet cakes.

Suzette had slept badly the night before, finally leaving Hyland and his grinding teeth to curl up on the couch in front of the TV and watch a few episodes of *Help Us, Nanny!* Other people's out-of-control lives—the shrieking children and untidy kitchens—soothed Suzette, making her feel both superior and sleepy. She admired Nanny Carolina and her smart chapeau.

Suzette scratched her forehead with her knuckle, the latex glove cool on her skin. She'd ordered an extra shot in her Starbucks Espresso Macchiato, but still felt foggy. "What is it, Leslie?" she said, her voice sharper than she'd intended.

"Hyland's on the phone," said Leslie, hands still waving like a showgirl's. "He says it's very important!"

Hyland was meeting Dorrie at the clinic for her pregnancy test; surely, he was calling with big or crushing news. Suzette hesitated, trying to ignore an excitement that felt more like terror than elation. From the OR, the pulse oximeter continued its steady song.

Suzette was scheduled to repair a ventricular septal defect in a nine-month-old boy named Camillo. Camillo had brown curls and a gummy smile. He was already sedated, the oxygen mask strapped over his face, an IV tube snaking across his wrist.

"Suzette?" said Brendan, the anesthesiologist. "We're ready for you now." Suzette didn't appreciate his tone.

"I'll be right there," she snapped. Over his mask, Brendan's eyes narrowed. Suzette had the highest surgery success rate at the hospital: she didn't always have to be pleasant. She didn't *ever* have to be pleasant. Though she usually was, or tried to be— Suzette cared deeply for her patients. She connected better with babies than with adults, especially now, now that each baby was a reminder, a flesh-and-blood manifestation of the mysterious promise that was possibly growing inside a girl from Galveston Island.

"What do you want me to tell him?" said Leslie. When Suzette didn't answer, Leslie blurted, "He's waiting for you on the phone!"

"Give me a minute," murmured Suzette. She sort of wanted another espresso, and sort of wanted a nap. She looked at Camillo, whose exposed chest was pale ocher, the color of Suzette and Hyland's dining room walls.

Camillo's mother had been a wreck. The day before, after Suzette had explained the early-morning procedure, Camillo's mother had thanked Suzette for taking special care of her baby, clutching Suzette's lab coat.

"Get some sleep," Suzette had counseled.

"Can I ask one thing?" Camillo's mother had implored, not letting go of the fabric.

"Of course," Suzette had said, smiling in what she hoped was a patient manner, though she was actually in a huge hurry, due for one more operation and then a party for Meg's birthday.

"If he dies . . . I'm just asking you," said Camillo's mother.

"Ruth . . ." said her husband, his voice carrying a weary warning.

"I'm allowed," said Camillo's mother. Camillo, finished with his bottle of milk and ready to play, squirmed in his mother's grasp, grinning maniacally at Suzette. How could she help but smile back? She sat down in the empty chair, silently apologizing to Meg, because she was going to be late (or entirely miss) her best friend's fortieth-birthday dinner.

"I'm listening," said Suzette. Camillo opened a pudgy palm, and Suzette extended her finger. He grasped it tightly.

"If something happens, and Camillo—"

"Nothing's going to happen, Ruth!" said Camillo's father.

"Let me finish. I'm not going to be there, in the operating room. But you will, Dr. Kendall—you will be there."

"Yes," said Suzette. "I will be there." She *would* be there for the surgery, though not for the post-op care. It was a delicate procedure, closing a hole in a plum-size heart. She utilized a needle as thin as an eyelash.

"If he's . . . slipping away, if he's going to die," said Camillo's mother, staring intently at Suzette, her brow a nest of lines, "I just want to ask you to say, just to whisper to him, to Camillo, just whisper, *May the angels show you the way to Heaven.*"

"Oh," said Suzette, sitting back in her chair. She thought, *Really? Angels?* Suzette's mother had always talked about angels.

"Tell him I'll be there as soon as I can," said Camillo's mother.

Suzette was overcome. She believed in none of it—not angels, not God—she believed in working your ass off and never making mistakes. But Camillo's mother's penetrating gaze, the strength of the baby's hold on her finger.

"I promise," she said, uncomfortably.

• • •

"Dr. Kendall?" said Brendan. Suzette blinked, brought herself back to the present. "Are we ready, Dr. Kendall?" said Brendan.

"But Hyland said it's *important*," Leslie repeated, raising her eyebrows. "We can page Dr. Liebovitz if you need to go." Leslie had often (and inappropriately) sent Suzette emails about "finding time for yourself" and "nurturing your marriage." A single woman with twin cats, she was inordinately concerned with Suzette's personal life (or lack thereof). Did she send Phil Liebovitz emails about nurturing his marriage?

Suzette swallowed. "Tell Hyland I'll call him back," she said, and she turned and walked toward Camillo. "*Led Zeppelin II*," she instructed Pam.

"All right," said Brendan approvingly.

Suzette ignored him. She closed her eyes and breathed in once, allowing herself a moment of worry—*Hyland said it's important*—and then breathed out, focusing completely on the task at hand. Robert Plant's voice overwhelmed her, shut down her chattering mind, as she knew it would. Time stopped, and Suzette's instinct took over. "We ready to go?" she asked.

"I'm good," said Brendan.

"Start time 0754," said Suzette. She picked up the knife and cut deeply into Camillo's chest.

Suzette and Pam worked quickly, exposing Camillo's thumping, maroon heart. Pam, as always, was steady and calm. The main pulmonary artery would give Suzette a good approach to the VSD, working across the pulmonary valve. With the tiny tools—Hyland had once joked that Suzette repaired hearts with tweezers—she inserted cannulas, tubes that would direct Camillo's blood out of his body to the heart-lung machine that would take over for the course of the operation so that Camillo's heart could rest and his lungs deflate.

Suzette fixed tourniquets to hold the cannulas in place, then sliced into the left atrium.

"The vent is on?" asked Suzette.

"The vent is on," said Pam.

Suzette could see bright red blood coming back from the left atrium. As his body cooled, Camillo's heart decompressed and stopped bleeding. Suzette made a hole in the main pulmonary artery so she could look down the valve and identify the VSD.

Camillo's heart slowed and grew still. Suzette always felt a sense of awe seeing a heart in this state: so vulnerable and easily manipulated. Pam suctioned carefully. Suzette pushed the valve leaflet out of the way, using stitches to hold the pulmonary artery. Splayed open, Camillo's heart was a pale orchid.

Carefully, Suzette lowered the endoscopic camera into the valve. While Suzette examined the images, Pam silently neatened the tools.

It was time to patch the VSD. Suzette stitched rapidly, using a running suture. "Ramble On" began playing, the slow strumming a perfect accompaniment to her work. She had to be careful—so careful—not to touch the aortic valve leaflets.

Ah, sometimes I grow so tired. Suzette let herself be carried by the song, by the precise movement of her fingers, almost as if they controlled her and not the other way around. This was the key to being a good (even great?) surgeon: not allowing yourself to know how much was at stake with every movement, the ability to become a perfect machine. In fifteen minutes, the hole was patched, all the leaflets still moving freely. Suzette breathed out. "Begin rewarming the patient," she said.

She took out the stay stitches, released the tourniquet to fill Camillo's heart with blood and de-air it. Suzette massaged air out of the pulmonary veins gently, Camillo's organ saggy and cold under her fingertips.

"Infuse the catheter with carbon dioxide," said Suzette. "And turn off the music."

Pam shuffled to the stereo, stopped Robert Plant mid-yowl.

The only sound in the room was the oximeter, its beeps like the final drops of a thunderstorm. Oxygenated blood entered Camillo's coronary arteries. Suzette lost her focus—just for an instant, thinking of Hyland, of Dorrie's eager smile. But then she shook her head and watched Camillo's chest. Pam had carefully folded navy blankets and laid them over his body, leaving only his sleeping face and the raw square around his surgical site exposed.

They waited. Camillo's heart was dark and silent.

Please, thought Suzette. It wasn't like her, and she wasn't even sure whom she was pleading with. She had a sudden memory of her mother, hysterical, covering the windows with black construction paper and telling Suzette to be silent lest they be caught and punished. *Please,* Suzette had prayed then as well, a girl just hoping for someone to *please* save her from her mother.

There was no need to pray. Suzette had performed the surgery without a flaw. And there—there! The baby's heart beat once, and again, and again. Suzette had brought him to the brink of death, then back to brilliant life.

Oxygenated blood turned Camillo's heart pink. Suzette removed the cannulas, put a warm sponge on Camillo's heart so it would not dry out while he rewarmed. She told Pam to call the echo team and confirm the repair.

"Cardiopulmonary off," said Suzette.

"Cardiopulmonary off," confirmed Pam.

Suzette used stainless-steel wire with an anesthetic catheter to sew Camillo's chest closed. When she was finished, she sighed audibly.

"Nice work," said Brendan.

Suzette did not answer. She exited the theater, rushed into her office, and called Hyland. He picked up on the first ring. "Where've you been?" he said.

"In surgery," said Suzette. "What is it?"

"Well," said Hyland. "Well, it worked. On the first round. She's pregnant. Dorrie's pregnant. We're pregnant. Suze. We're having a baby!"

8

Why in God's name had they chosen Chez Nous for their celebra-
tory dinner with Dorrie? What with the candles, the low music,
and the mustachioed waiter who made every dish sound sexy,
Suzette felt as if she was watching her husband on a date. A date
with a young woman carrying his baby. Because, in point of fact,
she *was* watching her husband on a date with a young woman
carrying his baby.

Dorrie looked around the plush restaurant, eyes shining. "You
know what?" she said, putting her small, plump hands on either
side of her bread dish. "I think it's a girl."

"A daughter!" cried Hyland. His gaze locked with Dorrie's as
he spoke, but he recovered quickly after the momentary lapse,
planting a kiss on his wife's cheek.

"Well, nothing's for sure until the sonogram, of course," said
Suzette. Hyland glared at her. "But a boy *or* a girl would be great!"
she added, her tone so awkward and high-pitched in her ears that
she wanted to cry.

"A daughter," said Dorrie, her fingers near Hyland's on the red
tablecloth, her eyes upon him.

"Someone is having a baby?" said the waiter, sidling up. (He
pronounced it with an accent: Zomeone eez having a *bébé?*)

"Yes, we are!" said Hyland.

"*Félicitations,*" said the waiter, his eyes darting from volup-tuous Dorrie to Suzette, her hair up, diamonds in her ears. "Lucky man," the waiter said, shrugging.

"So lucky," said Hyland. He wasn't a dope, but he thought Su-zette was more self-confident than she was.

"I'll have another kir royale," said Suzette.

"Of course," said the waiter. "And for the . . . ?" He halted, still unsure of the relationship geometry. "And *pour vous?*" he said, pointing to Dorrie.

"Sprite," said Dorrie, "thanks."

"If your hunch is right, and it's a girl," said Hyland, "what if we name her Eloise, after my sister?" Suzette had seen pictures of the serious girl, eleven when she was killed. She'd been a gifted ballerina, apparently.

"That's a pretty name," said Dorrie tepidly.

Suzette couldn't think of one thing to say. She always thought if she had a daughter, she'd name her Amelia, after Amelia Ear-hart.

"Perfect," said Hyland. He didn't seem to notice Suzette's si-lence. The drinks arrived, and Suzette tilted her glass and filled her mouth with currant-flavored bubbles, then swallowed, wait-ing for some sort of euphoria to kick in.

After a trio of desserts, Hyland paid the bill. Outside the res-taurant, he opened the driver's-side door of Dorrie's car, repeated his thanks, and said, "See you at the clinic for the sonogram?"

"OK," said Dorrie, smiling up at Hyland. "I'll see you then."

When she had driven away, Hyland took Suzette in his arms. "It's really happening," he said, kissing her tenderly. "I can't be-lieve it. It's really happening."

Suzette tried to breathe in deeply, to "breathe through her fear," as her meditation cassette tape advised. She told herself her panic was misplaced, that she was safe, that everything would be fine. In Hyland's arms, she was warm.

They watched Dorrie's taillights grow smaller as she drove along Southmore Boulevard. She put on her blinker, waited. When the light changed to green, she turned left on San Jacinto, which fed to 59, then Interstate 45, heading south.

And then she vanished.

Part Two

———————

1

Dorrie

Why did I do it? This seems a fair question, and believe me, I've asked it of myself a million times. Why did I sign up to be a surrogate, to lease my body, growing a child to sell to Hyland and Suzette Kendall? The clinic tells you, by the way, that you will be compensated for your time and care . . . not for the baby. But it's the baby you're being paid for. Your baby.

You.

The answer is so simple it seems impossible: money, and all that money meant to me. It meant I could get off of Galveston Island, and I wanted this more than anything. It meant I could move away from my mother and her dull disappointment, away from stories about my deadbeat dad. It meant a bigger life: college, a chance to be amongst other people for whom books were more important than food.

When I saw the billboard advertisement for the Fertility Clinic of Houston, I was working at Sea-O-Rama feeding penguins. It was as awful as it sounds, standing inside a chilled glass enclosure shoveling iced fish from a barrel to the ground, spreading the carcasses around so every ravenous penguin could have a taste. The memory of waking up with that manky smell of penguins in my hair—no matter how many times I washed it—still makes me queasy.

The Fertility Clinic of Houston told me I'd trade nine months of my life—nine months of reading in bed and eating healthy foods, which some intended parents would even *pay for*—for $35,000. It was enough for one year at absolutely any college in the state (Rice University!), and four years at some. I'd earned $5.60 an hour at Sonic, where I worked all through high school. I earned $8.40 an hour at Sea-O-Rama. My mother, who had sold concessions to aquarium goers for nine years, made $12 an hour. I added it up on my desk calculator: it would take two years to earn the same amount—521 days (working five days a week) of fending off those vicious, feral rats of the sea (as I called them in my mind). Four thousand one hundred and sixty-eight hours. And by the way, an hour of feeding penguins feels like 17 million hours.

Or I could sign the papers, give the gift of life, and be free. The equation seemed simple and life-changing. I signed.

And then, as planned, you were conceived after many painful shots and one round of clinical injections. You began to grow inside me. Almost instantly, I understood that the equation had been wrong. I had forgotten the most important factor, and that was you.

I loved you months before I felt your fluttering kicks, before I saw your fierce, red face. I loved you more than the idea of college, more than the scraps of possible lives I'd allowed myself to imagine. All of these future selves—Dorrie the professor, in a shaded office lit by a single lamp; Dorrie the writer, living in a California cottage; Dorrie the librarian, shelving books on cool, rainy days—they would all be ruined without you.

It sounds melodramatic, I know! I was so young, you have to

understand, only twenty-one. My mother might have been capable once, but discontent had turned her sour, made her into someone so unhappy it hurt to be in the house together. I had tried to help her, planting pamphlets about treating depression and making healthy meals. Nothing seemed to do any good. I couldn't change the fact that my father had left, taking her zest for life right along with him.

I knew it was you I'd been waiting for from the very start, from the first morning I felt deeply ill and understood. But you didn't belong to me; the papers I'd signed were clear. In the state of Texas, you could never be mine.

Maybe running away was the truest thing I ever did. Maybe it was the worst mistake of my life.

I walked out of the fancy French restaurant where the Kendalls had taken me for dinner. I put my hand on my stomach, which was still flat . . . you were only the size of a pea! I would have seen you on the sonogram at the next appointment—that would have explained a lot—but I didn't need to know any more. My choice was plain: I could stay, and give you to Hyland Kendall (at the moment I decided, he was standing with his arm around Suzette, waving as I drove away. I knew he'd be a great father, that was never the question. And Suzette . . . what can I say? She was wound as tight as a fist, but she was not unkind). I could take the money and step forward into a life I now knew would be incomplete, a black hole at its center, the missing space of you. Or I could pack what little I cared about into a suitcase and run.

I took a deep breath. The Houston night was too bright. In many other states, the papers I'd signed would not be valid. I could get out of Texas and we would be together. You would never even need to know where you had come from. It was love versus money, in the end, my dear baby girl.

I chose love.

2

Suzette

On the morning of Dorrie's sonogram, Suzette woke up to find Hyland at the foot of their bed, holding a tray with coffee and sliced melon. "Good morning!" he said. "I brought you breakfast! In bed!" His voice was both manic and thrilled.

Suzette sat up, rubbed her eyes. "I haven't slept this late since our honeymoon," she said. "What time is it? Eight? This is *glorious*. And breakfast in bed, thank you, honey."

"Thanks for taking the morning off," said Hyland.

Suzette nodded. It hadn't been easy, but Hyland had made it clear how important it was that they both be in the obstetrician's office when they saw the baby onscreen for the first time. Hyland radiated happiness, and Suzette felt... well... unsettled. And compounding her unsettledness was the sense that she *should* be radiating happiness, too. And she should be reading the books about motherhood that Hyland was leaving on her bedside table. And she should have opinions about the crib, the bumper, and the nursery glider, whatever the hell a *nursery glider* was. (Suzette had once held a *sugar glider*, a tiny flying opossum, but she knew the two were unrelated.)

In all honesty, although she was grateful for Dorrie's egg and womb, Suzette was already growing weary of their complicated triangle. It wasn't easy to see Hyland so joyous about creating a life with a younger woman (and one clearly besotted). Suzette wasn't threatened, of course ... although, OK, maybe she was. She was ready for Dorrie to be wheeled out of sight, like a donor body after harvest.

Hyland gave Suzette the tray and then hovered nervously, reminding her that they didn't want to be late.

"OK!" said Suzette. She showered and dressed, and they arrived at the doctor's office ten minutes before their 9:30 appointment. Suzette sat down while Hyland went to check in. He returned, frowning. "She's not here yet," he said.

"Calm down."

"Sorry. I'm just ... Ugh, this is hard. Our child just ... being driven around in a dented Mazda sedan."

"I know." She took his hand. Her pager beeped and she ignored it. They watched a morning news show. A woman in a bikini was teaching the anchor how to make a piñata. At 9:45, Hyland called Dorrie's house (she didn't have a cellphone). There was no answer, so he continued to call every ten minutes, reaching the morose answering machine each time: *Hello, you have reached Patsy and Dorrie Muscarello. We're not available right now. Please leave a message after the beep?*

They stared at the TV. At 10:30, an old episode of *The Love Boat* began. "We'd better go out there," said Hyland. "To Galveston."

"Do you think?" said Suzette.

He stood. "I can't just sit here," he said. "Where the hell is she?"

Suzette looked at her watch. "I really should . . ." she said. She had a full schedule starting at noon.

"Go ahead," he said. "I bet she just . . . slept through her alarm. Or forgot. Who knows? I'll go see what's happening," he said.

"OK," said Suzette. She felt calmer than she had in weeks. She kissed Hyland on the cheek and said, "Keep me posted." He nodded, agitated, dialing Dorrie's house again.

Suzette was scrubbing in for her first operation of the day when Hyland called. Leslie held the phone to Suzette's ear. Hyland's voice was small. "She's gone," he said.

"Gone?" said Suzette. "What do you mean, *gone?*"

"She's run away," said Hyland. "She's kidnapped our baby."

"Dr. Kendall?" said Leslie.

"I'll call you back in a few hours," said Suzette. "I'm sure she'll show up, honey."

"She left a note for me. It was taped to her front door," said Hyland. "She says she's sorry. She says she's never coming back."

3

Dorrie

The morning of the sonogram had loomed large on my calendar; I'd told myself that by that day I had to make my final decision to stay put or escape. I knew that not showing up would trigger a manhunt. Suzette Kendall was not a woman you wanted to fuck with (pardon my French!).

I tried to confide in my mother, but when I told her the first part of the story—that I'd signed up to be a surrogate—she freaked out so completely that I didn't have the strength to continue. I should have known she'd never understand. As she'd told me many times, if she'd never gotten pregnant with me, my father might still be around. The concept of valuing a baby, protecting your daughter, cherishing her . . . these were not ideas that held any traction with Patsy Black Muscarello. Because of me, she'd lost her husband. That was her sorry tale. I felt for her, but I was going to create a totally different life. One built on love and security, on loyalty and kindness. I guess, in retrospect, I can see that I was trying to fix her mistakes in a way, to heal my own wounds of abandonment by holding on to you. But I guess that's the way the world works—you try to do better than your parents. Is that so wrong? Sometimes you succeed and sometimes you do not.

On the night before the big appointment, I could not sleep. I tossed and twisted, eventually opening my favorite book, *The Awakening* by Kate Chopin. (I bought it after seeing the movie.) I identified with Edna, the protagonist, despite her unfortunate, watery end.

Years before, I had underlined Mademoiselle Reisz's conversation with Edna in my hardback copy of the book:

"And, moreover, to succeed, the artist must possess the courageous soul."

"What do you mean by the courageous soul?"

"Courageous, ma foi! The brave soul. The soul that dares and defies."

In the middle of the night, my favorite book spoke to me. I wanted to be a brave soul. It seemed so clear: I would drive away from Texas and make a life on Grand Isle, Louisiana!

It took no time at all to pack pajamas, a few favorite outfits, prenatal vitamins, and some novels to keep me from feeling lonely. My mother's snoring anchored the house to the ground. I felt light as I started my car and drove away, the *Texas Atlas & Gazetteer* on my lap. Your father had bought and mailed me the tome after I'd been late to my insemination appointment. There had even been a note in the package: *Hope this is helpful! Warmly, Hyland & Suzette.*

Warmly! The worst salutation in the book, as bloodless as *Sincerely Yours* or *Best Wishes* but with an added edge of sleaze. Still, I had taken a bottle of Wite-Out from my desk, erased Suzette's name, and put the note in my bedside table.

The drive to Grand Isle would take over six hours, which seemed tiring but possible. For you, I would forgo my favorite pick-me-up, Diet Coke. (I have never liked coffee. I like sweet things—soda and toffee peanuts. Do you?)

I let myself fall into a reverie as I drove, trying to imagine my entirely new life. A cottage on an isle. My daughter—you—with coltish legs and small, pink sneakers. A job at a quiet seaside restaurant, or maybe a bookstore? A new diary in which to write. A new library card, one for us to share. I could buy a little basket and fill it with sunscreen and bug spray. Plastic water wings, when you were old enough to swim. Maybe a porch, a sleeping porch, with a swing where we could read.

Somehow, I knew you were a girl, and that I would name you Zelda. The Kendalls' name for you was Eloise, after your father's dead sister. So sad! His whole family had been killed in a car accident, leaving him alone at age eleven. It had been this story that had drawn me to him, during our initial meeting at the Yo Ho Ho. This story and his seersucker pants, the first I had ever seen worn by a man who was not in a movie. The pants made me think of F. Scott Fitzgerald, and then, of course, of his wife, Zelda. (In addition to novels, I read biographies, the wilder the better.)

It was the perfect name for you. You would be tempestuous, impossible to resist, powerful. You would be everything I wished I could be.

4

Suzette

The police department had told the Kendalls to call back after twenty-four hours to file a missing persons report. When Suzette was finished for the day, she and Hyland drove to the Fertility Clinic of Houston, where Margaret, the secretary, agreed that this was an unfortunate development but reminded Suzette that they were not legally responsible for this (or any) situation arising outside the specific instances outlined in the multitudinous forms that Hyland and Suzette had signed. Also, Margaret noted, the office should have closed at six, and she was truly sorry, but they had to go home, or if not home, elsewhere.

Suzette slid into a heightened state that felt familiar—as a girl, she'd come home many times to be completely shocked by what her mother's mind had wrought: new couches delivered; a teenage boy in his underpants, eating Froot Loops; a gun Suzette's mother insisted they needed to protect themselves against the government or alien abductors. After a while, Suzette's fear just sort of . . . burned out, and she approached her childhood home on Chokecherry Lane with a measured calm, ready for anything.

"What have we done?" said Hyland.
"It's under control," Suzette muttered.
"Under control?" said Hyland.
"I'm truly sorry," said Margaret, jangling the office keys.
"We get it," said Suzette. "We're leaving."

The drive from the fertility clinic to their Bellaire home took half an hour. Hyland almost rear-ended a Jaguar getting off the interstate, and when Suzette shrieked, Hyland pulled the car over. "I'm not feeling very well," he said.

"Oh, OK, I can drive," said Suzette. "You want me to drive?" This was—in their fifteen years of marriage—the first time Hyland had ever asked her to take over the wheel. Even when he was tipsy, he insisted he was fine. Suzette had been in a number of fender-benders and one big accident, totaling her grad school Honda turning left when she didn't have the right-of-way, so she was usually more than happy to sit in the passenger seat.

But now Hyland nodded. Suzette looked over her shoulder as she walked around the car to reach the driver's seat. On the wall opposite, someone had used spray paint to write NEVER GIVE UP under a row of Pac-Mans.

"Got to admire the sentiment," she commented, as she put the car in gear.

"What?" said Hyland.

"Never give up," said Suzette, pointing.

"Oh," said Hyland.

"It's going to be OK," said Suzette.

"I know."

Suzette turned left on Wesleyan, left on Essex, right on Drexel. Their elegant home was lit up, the sconces on either side of the grand front door blazing. Suzette pulled into the garage. The classical station played at low volume until Suzette cut the engine. Hyland did not move. "I'm gutted," he said. "That's the word. Gutted. I want . . ." He did not finish.

"Everything's going to be fine," said Suzette.

As she was pulling on her bathrobe later that night, Suzette's beeper went off. She called the hospital to listen to the report: a patient's oxygen saturation levels were dropping. Suzette approved the protocol, adding, "I'll be right there."

"You are *not* going in," said Hyland, from the bathroom, where he'd been brushing his teeth.

"Yes, Hyland, I am." Something changed in the air then; Suzette sensed it immediately. She turned toward her husband, whose eyes were steely.

"Don't you feel anything?" he hissed.

"Hyland . . ."

"You don't care because it's not your fucking baby," said Hyland.

Suzette went cold. "I don't think you mean that," she managed.

"You're right," said Hyland, his shoulders caving forward as the venom seeped from him. "I don't mean that. I'm sorry." He sat down on their bed. "I just don't see how you can leave . . . not knowing where she is . . ."

"What good does it do for me to be here?" said Suzette.

"I know," said Hyland. His awful retort had taken the last of his energy.

Suzette took Hyland's hand. It was chilly, his fingers limp. His wedding ring had once been his own father's—Suzette had balked at his wearing the ghoulish gold band, which had been salvaged from the wreckage after the accident, but Hyland had insisted. He was sentimental, which she loved about him, but she saw now how sentimentality could lead to ineffectiveness, could make Hy-

land maudlin and lethargic when action was required. No matter:
Suzette was strong enough for the both of them.

"I'm sorry," said Hyland.

"It's OK."

"It's not OK. The baby's just as much yours as mine, and I'm
sorry."

He looked old, her Hyland, in his rumpled pajamas. Suzette
remembered a night in Paris, during their honeymoon, when
they had wandered the city for hours, stopping in for a drink or
snack at cafés they came across. Hyland still smoked then, and he
was thin and shining, speaking passable French. He had friends
in Paris from the year he'd studied abroad. Suzette, a hick from
upstate New York, was giddy with possession: she couldn't believe that this genius, this artist, was hers.

Now, his eyes were red, his face lined. Despite his weekly adult
ice hockey league (he'd been a right wing in college), he had a
sake belly. Had she made him helpless somehow, by taking such
care?

"She's just as much mine as she is yours," echoed Suzette. Hyland leaned over and pulled her toward him. He smelled like tomato soup. Why did he smell like tomato soup? For a moment,
resting her head against her husband's chest, Suzette felt like a
scared girl again, unsure of what the rules were, not knowing
how to proceed and if she'd ever feel normal, like the kids on *The
Cosby Show* or *Family Ties*, joking around with parents who didn't
seem to need taking care of.

5

Dorrie

I was the only person on Louisiana Highway 1. I sighed with relief upon seeing a sign reading WELCOME TO GRAND ISLE—
WHERE EVERY DAY IS AN ADVENTURE! The quiet town, decimated
every few years by one hurricane or another, was definitely the
end of the line, the place where Highway 1 ran into the gulf. I
cruised along the potholed road—almost underwater in some
sections—until I spotted a gas station, pulling in. I was ravenous
and so tired I felt as if I were drunk.

I wasn't, of course, and never would be. My mother's drinking
and depression had made me a teetotaler for life. This is something you should know: you have demons in your genes. Stay
away, far away, from booze or whatever else. I hope you'll never
know how sadness can twist your heart, and make you a stranger
to yourself. And seeking numbness only makes it worse. By the
time I reconnected with your grandmother, she was a missing
person, sitting right there in my childhood house on K½ Street.
Even over the phone, her ghostly voice made me furious and
scared.

But back to the story. In Grand Isle, I asked a convenience store clerk about nearby hotels.

"Sure," said the clerk, holding up fingers as he counted options. "There's the Cajun Holiday Motel, the Sandpiper Shores, Ricky's RV Park, the Seahorse Cottages . . ."

"The Seahorse Cottages," I said, liking the cheerful name. I picked out Twinkies, Combos, mixed nuts, gum, and another Sprite. I had stolen four hundred dollars from my mother's underwear drawer, and was giddy with freedom and what seemed to me like wealth.

The Seahorse, a motley collection of wooden structures on stilts, seemed deserted. I rang the bell outside what seemed to be an office. After a few minutes, a woman with white hair wearing an oversize T-shirt that read CAJUN FISHING RODEO 1989 came to the door, rubbing her eyes. "Ma'am?" she asked, stifling a yawn with her palm.

I asked to rent a cottage.

The woman narrowed her eyes. "You in trouble?" she asked.

I allowed that yes, I was.

The woman crossed her arms over her chest, considering. "Like man trouble?" she said, raising bushy eyebrows.

"Um, yes," I said, not lying, not exactly.

The woman held open the door. "Come on in," she said. "You'll be safe here." She handed me a key from the board behind the desk. She wore fuzzy slippers and her hair was gathered in a pink rubber band. "Cottage Three's open," she said. "Get some sleep."

I remember her kindness to this day.

Cottage 3 was run-down, the sagging bed covered in a garish comforter that clashed with the flowered shirt hung on a crooked rod above the bureau. There was a painting of a frightened-looking starfish, its one wide eye seeming to follow me around the room. The "kitchenette" was a microwave and a coffeepot, and when I pushed open the bathroom door, a roach scurried under the sink.

I lay down, already feeling badly for hurting your father and Suzette. I knew they must have been frantic. But I had simply not understood what it would feel like, back when I first walked into the Yo Ho Ho and saw the Kendalls—so perfect, like a storybook version of parents. They had stood, rising to greet me, and I had wanted to be their daughter myself.

In Cottage 3, I talked to you. I told you I could give you more than they could, though we'd never have a fancy house or a Lexus like the one Suzette drove. It seemed, however impossibly, that everything was going to work out. I had escaped my mother and her misery, and I was on an adventure like the ones I read about in the novels I loved.

I was the best English student at Ball High School. I want you to know that. I'm not badly educated or without grace. My spring semester, I thought I'd get a scholarship. I really thought that. But it turns out that being the best English student at a Galveston high school doesn't mean you don't have to pay for college. I was accepted to Rice, the so-called Harvard of Texas. But along with the jubilant letter and the glossy pictures came the tuition information. Even with loans, even with work-study, even if I lived under a tarp somewhere on campus, it was impossible. Getting into Rice University remains my greatest academic accomplishment.

Sometimes, when I see tourists come into Walgreens, smelling of expensive perfumes and chattering as if I'm not even there, ringing up their Advil or toothpaste, a part of me wants to scream, *I'm one of you! I almost went to Rice University!* But it isn't true. I'm not one of them. I'm a cautionary tale, a former teenage mother turned middle-aged, a woman who dyes her hair with Clairol and reads a book a week from the library, taking online classes in philosophy and British literature, clicking away on her old desktop Dell computer deep into the night, trying to make her brain stronger, trying to make up for four sun-dappled years on a campus she'd never even visit.

That's who I've become. Just so you know.

6

Suzette

Suzette drove to St. Luke's, turned in to the hospital garage, parked, and then sat in her car. Her hands shook as she brought them to her face. She needed a shower. She needed a coffee. Her beeper went off again.

Trembling, Suzette took her phone from her purse. She paused before entering the code to retrieve her messages. When she heard the report—her patient's stats were now normal, and he was resting comfortably—she dialed Meg. Her phone rang twice and then Meg answered, "Suzette?"

"Yeah."

"Have you found Dorrie?"

"No," said Suzette.

"Jesus H. Christ! I always knew there was something off about that girl. Sorry, I'm not saying the right things here."

Suzette managed a weary chuckle.

"Come over," said Meg. "No, wait, let's get pancakes. You know the IHOP on Westheimer?"

"Yes."

"What do you think? Or you could come here. Or do you want me to . . ."

"IHOP," said Suzette, starting her car. "I'm driving there right now."

"OK, me, too," said Meg. "Well, I need to change first. You should *see* this filthy outfit Stew got for our anniversary assignation."

"Leather?" asked Suzette.

"Pleather," said Meg. "I'm pro-animal, you know that." She was silent for a moment, and then said, "It's going to be OK, Suze."

"Is it?"

"Hyland sounded terrible when I called the house," said Meg.

"He's losing it," said Suzette.

"This is surreal," said Meg. "Some nut is pregnant with his baby . . . and now she's run off . . . it's like an episode of *Law & Order*. God, I'm sorry! Again, not saying the right things . . ."

Suzette had stopped listening. She should check on her patients. She should prep for her meeting about the Fletcher boy. She should go home and hold her husband. Normally decisive, she sat paralyzed, unable to put the car in reverse or park. "I don't know what to do," she said.

"I'm out of my pleather sex suit," said Meg. "I'm walking to my car."

"I should go to work," said Suzette. To speak about the Fletcher boy, she had to be completely composed.

"Work can wait," said Meg.

"It can't," said Suzette. Kevin Fletcher was going to rip her apart when she told him they were taking his son off the list. Suzette closed her eyes.

"But it will," said Meg. "I'm starting my engine. I'll see you in twenty."

"OK," said Suzette. She reversed her sedan and drove away from the hospital. She hadn't been to IHOP in years, but remembered every turn perfectly. The pancake house was a comforting sight in the predawn darkness, its awnings royal blue, its parking lot well lit and filled with a surprising number of cars.

Inside, Suzette saw Meg sitting at a corner booth. She felt her shoulders release as soon as Meg looked up and smiled. Suzette approached, and Meg stood. She'd tied her hair back and wore jeans with a blank white T-shirt. Meg pulled her close, and Suzette—embarrassing herself—went limp in Meg's arms, inhaling Meg's syrup-and-hairspray smell.

"Remember when we'd come here with Natasha?" said Suzette. Natasha was Meg's third daughter, and acid reflux had kept her up at all hours. Suzette had met Meg at IHOP after her late shifts. They'd pass baby Natasha between them, drink coffee, and eat.

"I do," said Meg. "How can she be in kindergarten?"

The waiter appeared with two coffees. "I'm sorry," said Suzette, "I haven't even looked at the menu."

"Got us two Rooty Tooty Fresh 'N Fruities," said Meg.

"You know me so well," said Suzette.

"OK," said Meg, touching Suzette's arm. "Just talk."

"There's this kid," said Suzette. She took a gulp of her coffee. "Martin Fletcher. He's very sick, getting worse. I performed his first operation, when he was a newborn. I shouldn't have become . . . close." She took a deep breath, put her head in her hands. "He needs a new heart, but he's no longer a strong candidate for a transplant. He's not a good risk. So I know they're going to take him off the list. I was hoping I could convince them, but I know . . . I can't."

"What list?"

Suzette sighed. "If a heart becomes available, it should go to someone who has a better chance of surviving."

"Fuck," said Meg. "So you're going to tell this kid's parents he's going to die?"

"We're all going to die," said Suzette, staring into her coffee.

"You always do accentuate the positive," said Meg drily.

"And also . . . Dorrie."

"Yes. Dorrie."

"She . . . she's just disappeared. She didn't show up for the sonogram, and, well, I guess she's run away or something."

"Oh, sweetie," said Meg. "I'm going to call my next-door neighbor. He works for KHOU News. They'll be all over this. Would that help?"

"I guess so. Why not?" Suzette said. The waiter returned with two plates of pancakes smothered in fruit compote and whipped cream.

"What else can I get for you lovely ladies?" he asked.

"We're fine," said Meg. "Thanks."

"This is so disgusting,' said Suzette, when the waiter was out of earshot.

"No joke," said Meg, digging in. "I'm going to have to run to Dallas and back to work this off."

Suzette's phone rang. She was afraid to check, but it was Hyland. "Honey," she said.

"I can't sleep," said Hyland.

"I'm at the IHOP on Westheimer with Meg."

"I'm coming over," said Hyland.

"OK, honey," said Suzette.

"Has the young runaway turned up?" asked Meg.

Suzette shook her head. "Where is she?" she said. "How can this be happening?"

"It's just a matter of time," said Meg. "They're going to find her, Suze. We're going to be sitting here tomorrow and every-thing will be fine. I promise."

"I already feel like the baby is mine," said Suzette, somewhat stunned to acknowledge this, even to herself. "I thought it would feel so great, Meg, but this is the worst."

"Welcome to parenthood," said Meg.

7

Dorrie

My first and only morning on Grand Isle, I slept for about an hour and then woke again, feeling sluggish and sick. Could this be morning sickness already? I pushed the curtains apart and took in my view of the Seahorse Cottages parking lot. A pickup truck idled and a floodlight illuminated the driver, a young man with a beard and a trucker cap. I pulled the drapes closed.

There was a phone on the desk. I gazed at it, almost calling my mom. I even lifted the receiver, but I did not dial. I couldn't bear to hear more disappointment in Patsy's voice.

My stomach growled so I ate the last of the Combos and a Twinkie. I turned on the television and was astonished to see my own face fill the screen. It was my high school yearbook photograph, my smile electric The anchorman spoke: "Dorrie Muscarello, last seen in Galveston, Texas, was known to friends and family as a nice person."

Suzette then appeared looking pale and composed, standing outside of an International House of Pancakes. What was Suzette doing at IHOP? Your father was slumped next to her. "If you can hear us, Dorrie," said Suzette, "please know we don't mean you any harm. We just want you home safe. Please, Dorrie. Don't make this any worse than it has to be. We beg you. We're going to find you, you know. Just turn yourself in." Suzette's voice veered between indignation and a slimy, false concern. "It's going to be OK, dear," she added. Was she speaking to me, calling me *dear*? For the first time, I hated her.

On the TV, Suzette turned to your father, who nodded. He managed, "That's right." His eyes were red-rimmed, his face puffy. There was little trace of the handsome man who had met me for breakfast before the first doctor's appointment, waving away my proffered dollars and telling me to "please, order a fancy coffee, too, on me. Order two!" He had been so happy, lit up with the possibility of you.

The young anchorman said that the Kendalls had offered a fifty-thousand-dollar reward for any information about my whereabouts. "She may have traveled out of state, or even out of the country, we just don't know," said a police officer. "She could be driving a silver Mazda sedan."

The segment concluded with a video shot outside my mom's bungalow in Galveston. The sky above the house was purple and marred with clouds. The newscaster wore a windbreaker. "Patsy Muscarello, a longtime resident of Galveston Island, refused to comment on her daughter's disappearance. Neighbors here on K½ Street say they always thought Dorrie was a nice girl who liked to help others. It seems they may have been wrong. For KHOU News, I'm Melissa Hornsbach."

I felt stung. Back in the studio, the news anchors were shaking their heads. Before they could condemn me further, I hit the mute button, understanding that I couldn't remain on Grand Isle. It was only a matter of hours before the motel owners would wake and recognize me. For all I knew, they were calling in their fifty-thousand-dollar reward at that very moment. Maybe the man in the truck was with the FBI, CIA, or whatever the organization was that would hunt down a defenseless young pregnant lady just trying to make a fresh start in the Seahorse Cottages!

I pulled on my jeans. Not bothering to lock the door behind me, I ran to the car. No one followed, and the truck remained where it had been, coughing exhaust. The man watched me drive out of the parking lot. I had dreamed for years of sitting by the waves that had inspired Kate Chopin. Instead, I was on the move again, heading north, toward New Orleans.

When I was on the outskirts of the city, I parked the Mazda outside a Wal-Mart Supercenter. I bought scissors and Pepperoni Pizza Cracker Combos. In a bathroom stall, I cut off all my hair. I stuffed the black curls I'd been so vain about into the maxipad receptacle. The tin box with hair coming out was a horror.

I did, however, look like a new person. A deranged and exhausted person, a person who had chopped off all her hair in the Wal-Mart bathroom stall and then stuffed it in the maxipad receptacle, but a new person nonetheless.

I ate the bag of Combos as I steered the Mazda into New Orleans. I felt as if I hadn't slept in days. I felt sick. I was worried that my desperation would harm you somehow. I chose an exit and got off the highway, found myself lost in a warren of streets. Whenever I slowed, figures approached—for a while, I wasn't sure if they were real or if I was going crazy. It was terrible.

I slowed for a red light, and a heavyset person in a miniskirt rapped at the driver's-side window. "Hey!" called the woman, whose face looked masculine, despite her cherry-red lipstick. "Hey! How about a ride?"

Scared, I hit the accelerator, drove straight through the red light, frantically trying to reach a more populated area. The EMPTY light blinked on the gas gauge. My entire body crackled with panic. When I finally reached Tulane Avenue again, I stayed on it, helplessly moving forward, hoping for a hotel or even a restaurant. I saw a po' boy shop, an open doorway surrounded by men in hooded jackets and hats.

Finally, a motel. A seedy motel, to be sure, with a hand-painted sign reading THE MOTEL CLAIBORNE, but it had a parking lot. I pulled into the lot and exhaled, reading the sign posted on the wall in front of my car:

NO REFUNDS

NO HOURLY RATES

NO PROSTITUTION

NO DRUGS

NO ADULT ENTERTAINMENT

NO SOLICITATION

NO LOITERING

The parking lot was busy—men and women in various stages of angry or blank inebriation. I walked quickly to the office, where a sign in Magic Marker read:

Wlecome to the Claiborne

1 bed $55.00/day

2 beds $65.00/day

The office was cluttered and dimly lit. A few men seemed to be hanging around, resting drinks on the massive mahogany front desk. This seemed (I told myself—and please remember, I was hungry, exhausted, possibly delusional, and so very worried about *you*) a good place to hide, a place where having secrets might be just fine.

A florid man wearing a button-down shirt and a thin tie asked me if I was checking in. I nodded, thinking fleetingly of Mary and Joseph searching for room at the inn. But the man did not send me to the manger. He nodded mildly and pushed a clipboard across the desk.

I stared at the form. The time had come, I thought grandly, to begin again. I could take the Bic pen that had been jammed into the clip and write down any NAME, ADDRESS, EMERGENCY CONTACT, and STATE OF RESIDENCE that I damn well pleased.

Well, I asked myself, who are you going to be?

I wrote that my NAME was Jardine. My ADDRESS was a P.O. box in Portland, Maine, the birthplace of another of my favorite writers, Stephen King. For an emergency contact, I fabricated a phone number.

"Credit card?" asked the man.

I told the man I would be paying cash.

The man hesitated, then shrugged. "One bed or two?" he asked.

I told him one bed was fine, calculating my wad of cash divided by the daily rate slowly and painstakingly in my head. Math! I had always hated math. (Ah, the irony: I have spent my days punching numbers into a Walgreens register.)

I opened my wallet, sensing a ripple of interest in the lobby. I counted out enough for five days, then handed over the bills. The man handed me a key to Room 29.

"Elevator's on your left there," said the man. "You've got a balcony and all."

I headed for the elevator. Was I safe? I didn't feel safe. In fact, were I the betting type, I would have put all my chips on NO I WAS NOT SAFE. (I am not the betting type.)

I punched the elevator button once, twice, three times. Finally, the small chamber appeared and I hustled inside. In moments, I was deposited on the second floor. I found Room 29 and unlocked the door. The room was small and not very clean. It was clear at this point that the Motel Claiborne was a flophouse, or however you want to put it. A drug den, a den of iniquity. I was inside a Dashiell Hammett novel, which would have been exciting in my previous life, when I was a girl from a small island looking for excitement. That girl would have been thrilled to spend a night in New Orleans. But now I was someone different. I was going to be your mother, and I wanted only peace and the ability to become my best self, for you.

There was no TV remote. I tried to turn on the TV by punching every single possible button, but nothing happened. I climbed on top of the bed, which exhaled duskily as I sank into the wrinkled coverlet. Oh, we were so very tired. We slept.

8

Suzette

After pancakes, Suzette went home with Hyland for a few sleep-
less hours, then showered and went to work. Hyland saw her
off, unshaven, eyes bruised. Their neighbor, elderly Rhonda
Bardwell, paused, watering can midair, when Suzette stepped
outside. An army of landscapers arrived every day to maintain
Rhonda's elaborate yard, yet there she stood in a threadbare robe
and slippers, caring for the potted fern situated next to her front
door.

"Morning," said Suzette.

"Why, good *morning*," said Rhonda, her tone making it clear
she had seen the news reports, which had (in retrospect) been a
mistake, serving only to violate the Kendalls' privacy without
yielding any credible leads. Rhonda, an oil widow with two red-
faced sons who lumbered by occasionally, surrounded by swarms
of children and wives who appraised the decaying mansion and
its contents with their eyes, arranged her face expectantly, her
forehead rising in anticipation of an update.

But Suzette did not deliver, turning from Rhonda and Hyland

and walking to the Lexus, which she had parked out front due to the garage being filled with cardboard boxes. "Can you put the boxes out?" she called to Hyland.

He nodded. Suzette guessed he would spend the day sitting by the phone, continuing to catalog the dusty contents of his childhood home. She knew that Dorrie's disappearance was another devastating blow to her husband, who had come so far since the accident that had defined him. Suzette understood his desire to replace what had been taken away. To—quite literally, as it turned out—fill his sister's shoes. (He'd placed a box of worn ballet slippers in the baby's closet.) Suzette had problems herself—she forgave and accepted Hyland in total. She loved him for trying to find happiness, rather than giving up hope. Being married to a man who cared too much was an issue Suzette was happy to have. She could only imagine that their child, if they ever had one, would agree.

Suzette got into the Lexus as Rhonda stared, her narrowed gaze a dam holding back a river of opinions. Suzette drove away, glad to be free from the miserable cocoon she and Hyland had made around themselves—waiting for the phone to ring, watching the TV on mute, and slowly emptying a large bottle of sake.

Suzette knew nothing about classical music, but this didn't stop her from loving it. She enjoyed the absence of words, and tried to imagine what each song should be a soundtrack beneath: a mouse wedding, for example . . . a woodland dinner party, a battle on ice skates. As she drove to the hospital, Suzette thought idly that she and her someday-baby could play this game. *What does this song sound like?* Suzette would ask, and Eloise, from the backseat, would pipe, "A mouse wedding, Mommy!"

Suzette realized, alarmed, that she was about to cry. She rubbed her eyes with the back of her hand, blinked furiously. It was that word—*Mommy*. It did something to Suzette, made her fall apart. *Mommy*, a sappy yet beautiful word, conjuring home-made jam and sewing supplies; a lovely young woman in a kerchief kneeling down as a child ran across a wide lawn for a hug. Suzette tried to pull herself together. She'd never used a needle or pincushion in her life.

No one mentioned Suzette's missing surrogate or the news reports at the morning conference. Suzette made her case for Martin Fletcher, but the decision was data-driven: Martin was removed from the transplant list. After the weekly Morbidity and Mortality report, the day's surgeries were outlined. There was no place for small talk. Like many of her colleagues, Suzette was intensely private. Sure, they bantered here and there about golf handicaps or the weather, but their work was serious, an honor, and bridging the gap between chitchat and the intensity needed to saw open a breastplate took energy none of them could spare. It was a relief to be amongst her tribe.

Suzette had gone to medical school planning to be a pediatrician. But shortly into her rotation, she realized she found the work stultifying: viruses, well-child checkups, the biggest thrill a sprained wrist. When she mentioned idly to her attending, Bill Levine, that 90 percent of the patients seemed to have ear infections, he put down his coffee mug and looked at her.

"You're too aggressive," he said simply.

And while she'd heard this before, and always as an insult, Suzette had to agree. "Where, then?" she asked Dr. Levine. "ER?"

Levine sat back in his desk chair, tapped his pen against his lips. He narrowed his eyes, evaluating her. Then he nodded. "Cardiothoracic surgery," he said.

"Oh, yeah?" said Suzette. She felt an almost carnal thrill at the proclamation, though Levine was a grandfather with ear hair and a paunch.

"Yes," he said.

The air between them was electric. A heart surgeon was beyond her wildest dreams—the best of the best, the biggest boys' club, the alphas. Levine met Suzette's gaze, and she saw in him the dashing guy he must have been, before the years of vomiting children had reduced him to this. "Do it," he said.

Suzette nodded. She was twenty-nine. "I will," she said.

At 8:00 A.M., Suzette ate a bagel and peed (not knowing when she could do either again), then changed for her first operation, a transcatheter aortic valve replacement. She put on her headlight and loupes (the gear so heavy she was already starting to stoop forward like her older colleagues), then the rest of her equipment. She scrubbed in, counting down the seven minutes. Suzette paid special attention to the nail beds around her short fingernails; she hadn't worn polish since her wedding day.

Cassie, the scrub nurse, handed Suzette a sterile towel. Suzette pulled her gloves on, letting them snap tight with a flourish (it was a tough maneuver with even slightly wet hands). After the long night of confusion and misery, she was back. It was her *job* to forget about Dorrie. And yet she requested classical music, causing Cassie to look up at her, momentarily confused. Suzette kept a stack of CDs next to the player and rotated amongst them, rarely adding to the pile.

"The classical music station," said Suzette.

"I thought you—"

"Please," said Suzette, in a tone that was anything but questioning.

The TAVR was risky: Suzette would run a catheter the size of a pen from an artery in the leg to the heart, then implant a valve made of bovine tissue and supported on a metal stent. In a few hours, if all went well, the patient (a middle-aged, mildly famous newscaster named Graham Magnuson) would have a functioning aortic valve.

Cassie messed around with the radio, her anxious breath becoming audible. The OR was silent but for the scratchy progression of songs: country ballad, Spanish-language ballad, Bruce Springsteen singing, *Baby, we were born to run . . .*

Suzette inhaled sharply.

"I'm sorry," said Cassie, punching the radio. "I've got a Mozart tape in my office?"

"Dr. Kendall," said Brendan, goddamn Brendan, standing in the corner with his vials of sleep.

"Fine," said Suzette. *"Led Zeppelin II."*

Cassie sighed with relief. Suzette closed her eyes, saying goodbye to the mouse wedding, to all of it. She opened her eyes. "Incision," she said, opening her palm.

"Incision," said Cassie, handing her the knife.

After the TAVR, Suzette took a quick coffee break in her office, checking emails and dictating operative reports, then prepped for her 11:30 aortic valve replacement. She had told Hyland to call her with any updates, and he had not called. Leslie paused by her office door, leaning against the frame but not daring (not even Leslie) to come in. "Ummm?" she said, by way of greeting. Suzette continued typing an email.

"Ummm?" said Leslie, rapping the door with her knuckle. "Ummm, Dr. Kendall?"

"Yes?" said Suzette, not looking away from the computer screen.

"Ummm, there are reporters outside."

Suzette sighed and turned to Leslie. "Don't let them in," she said.

"Oh no! Of course I wouldn't! Goodness, no. I just thought you . . ."

Suzette went back to her email.

". . . would want to know," said Leslie.

Suzette had finished the note—it was a quick response to a patient who was feeling short of breath—but she continued to peck at the keys, wishing Leslie away, typing, *GO AWAY LES-LIE GO AWAY LESLIE.*

"Well, just so you know, I'm really praying for you," said Leslie.

GET OUT OF MY DOORWAY LESLIE, Suzette typed. "Thanks so much," she said.

"Ummm?" said Leslie.

"I'll be out in a minute," said Suzette.

When Leslie finally moved on, Suzette shut her office door. She massaged her temples. She went to Amazon.com and ordered some Beethoven and Chopin and Eric Satie. She heated up a ramen noodle bowl in her microwave, ate it while evaluating patient charts. And then she went into the locker room to change.

At 11:30, Suzette scrubbed in again. The patient was an elderly woman, Judith Rabinowitz, who'd told Suzette she'd been taken from her parents by Nazi troops. "I never saw my parents again," said Judith, sitting up in her hospital bed. She was surrounded by her husband, three daughters, and five grandchildren. "I was *Germanized*," she told Suzette emphatically. "That's what they called it. But I wasn't *Germanized* enough!"

At this, Judith's husband, a handsome brown-haired man with thick glasses, guffawed. He patted her hand. "Take care of my Judy's heart," he said to Suzette. "We have a trip to Warsaw planned for next spring."

"I'm in it for the Danube cruise afterward," confided Judith. "Unlimited buffet."

"Oh, Mom," said one of Judith's daughters.

"I've heard they have crab claws," said Judith dreamily.

Suzette had begun to describe the operation, but Judith held up her palms like a traffic cop. "Spare me," she said. "I know you'll do your best."

Suzette smiled, and opened her mouth to say something—some reassuring platitude—but a grandson interrupted her, hurling himself from the foot of the bed into Judith's arms.

"Abraham!" cried his mother. But Judith held up her hand again, letting the boy nuzzle close.

Now, Judith was sedated and prepped. Suzette entered the operating room, forgetting to ask for any music at all, and began. Hours later, when the mechanical valve was in place, Suzette changed and poured coffee. She shut her office door firmly and called Hyland, who sounded morose.

"No word," he said.

"I figured," said Suzette, pressing her fingertips into her forehead where the headlight bore against her skull, leaving a dent and residual pain.

"What should I do?" said Hyland.

"I'm not going to call again," said Suzette. "If you need anything, or if there's news, call me."

"I'm sorry," said Hyland. "I know you're busy. I'll make veal for dinner."

"Veal?" said Suzette.

"I don't know why I said that. Do you like veal?"

"I don't know. Sure."

"OK, forget veal. Just forget veal!"

"Are you going back to work?" asked Suzette.

"Work? How could I?" said Hyland.

Suzette bit her lip, but didn't answer.

• • •

Her third operation of the day was a coronary bypass. The patient, a heavyset postal worker named Phillip Varnado, was unconscious by the time Suzette scrubbed in, a nurse anesthetist named Karen Lawrence at his side. The ventilator wheezed. Karen glanced at Suzette and nodded, then looked back down and adjusted the patient's isoflurane. Although they'd crack the sternum to get access to the heart, the CBA did not require a heart-lung machine.

"You choose," said Suzette, when Leslie paused by the CD player. Leslie (as could be expected) chose *Guys and Dolls.* Show tunes! Karen caught Suzette's gaze, rolling her eyes playfully. It was a weird job, anesthetist—controlling a patient's consciousness, re-jiggering his memories, even erasing pain retroactively. If Suzette ever wrote a murder mystery, she'd confided to Hyland, she'd make the serial killer an anesthesiologist. "You could do *anything* to a patient," Suzette had said, "and then make them forget it!"

"Fucking creepy," Hyland had said. Suzette had laughed and agreed.

To the strains of "Luck Be a Lady," Suzette got to work, incising a clean line down the chest, then calling for the sternal saw. Her throbbing headache and the pain in her lower back faded as she worked to expose Varnado's diseased heart. She could operate for hours, completely focused. One of her few female colleagues had gone into full-blown labor while operating and hadn't even realized it—she'd been rushed to the maternity ward upon completing the procedure.

The left anterior descending coronary artery and right coronary artery were obstructed. Suzette stabilized the heart and prepared to harvest the bypass grafts from the saphenous vein in Varnado's leg. Leslie hummed along to the song, some god-awful dirge—"Follow the Fold." Suzette felt dizzy, and took a few deep breaths.

"Are you OK?" asked Leslie.

Suzette nodded, but she saw Dorrie's flushed face whenever she blinked. What the hell? She'd never been distracted like this before.

"Dr. Kendall?" said Leslie.

"I'm fine," said Suzette, forcing Dorrie and the baby from her mind and harvesting the vein grafts. "Heparin," she said.

"Heparin," said Leslie.

Suzette's tools were ready. She breathed evenly, sewing one end of each vein graft onto the coronary arteries beyond the obstructions, then attaching the other end to the aorta. The first graft went perfectly, but Suzette slipped during the second, piercing the vein with her scalpel, rendering it useless. "Fuck!" she said.

She looked up. Karen's eyes above her mask were concerned. Suzette had to go back and reharvest another vein. "It's this damn music," said Suzette.

"I'm sorry," said Leslie, turning it off. In silence, Suzette completed the surgery without incident. When she finished, and Varnado was wheeled from the room, Leslie hovered nearby.

"Happens to everyone," said Karen.

"Not to me," said Suzette.

"Turned out fine," said Karen, pulling off her gloves and exiting.

"Well, I can only guess what you must feel like," interjected Leslie. "You must be scared to death."

Suzette sighed. "I don't want you to mention the . . . situation again," she said.

"Well, my word!" said Leslie.

"Thank you," said Suzette.

Changing out of her scrubs, Suzette went over her cases in her mind. She'd always suspected, deep inside, that to do her job well took all of her, all she had.

For a split second, though of course she wanted them to find Dorrie, Suzette let herself envision a life without a child. Sunsets with a good bottle of Malbec. Lazy Sundays, making love and going to galleries. Extended vacations to exotic locales. Hyland really *seeing* Suzette again, the way he once had—as opposed to treating her as a pal, someone with whom he could discuss the exterminator bill. Was it possible that Dorrie, wherever she had gone, could give the baby a good life? A better life, maybe, than Suzette?

9

Dorrie

Until my time in New Orleans, every day of my life had always ended with a book. But as the days in the Motel Claiborne passed, hot and stultifying, something seemed to go wrong in my brain: I couldn't read. I had two paperbacks in my knapsack, but neither *Endless Love* nor *Love Story* provided relief.

I saw each individual word. But I never fell through the words into the story. I'd never dwelled on the mechanics of reading before—it just *worked*, subconsciously, like breathing. I would open a book, fall through the words, and exist in an alternate universe. Once, after a *60 Minutes* episode condemning solitary confinement in prisons, I'd said to Patsy, "How bad could it be? You could just read all day." My mother had made that clucking sound (half bemusement, half condemnation) and refilled her wineglass.

I was overcome by paranoia, terrified every time I left the room, certain that someone would recognize me and turn me in. I hoarded snacks from the vending machine down the hall: peanuts, granola bars, cookies, gum. My cash supply dwindled, and my mind was overtaken by worries and what-ifs.

What if someone reported my car? How was I going to pay for more time at the Motel Claiborne? If I used a credit card, I'd be found. I was probably all over the news—if I ventured into the city, I'd be identified, I was sure of it. And though I was not breaking the law, I was frightened of your father and Suzette's power.

I tied myself in mental knots trying to formulate a plan. Days and then a week went by. Room 29 was horrible. The window unit rumbled loudly but didn't seem to cool the stifling air. The room smelled of urine and a pungent, salty smell that was undeniably (and revoltingly) sexual. Besides the broken TV, Room 29 had a bedside table with a glued-shut drawer, a large mirror I didn't want to peer into, and the single bed, which was still covered with the cheap, rumpled sheets I'd discovered on my first night.

The sun shot through the window like a hot fist. I was so tired, too tired. My head began to ache no matter how much water I drank from the sink. My nose was clogged and my throat felt parched. When I swallowed, it felt as if there were knives in my throat. My joints ached and I shivered with a chill I was afraid meant I had a fever.

I was so low I decided I would call my mother. Though she had never understood me—what I wanted, who I was—she was the only one I could think to reach out to. I'd always been a loner. The other girls in school thought *I thought* I was better than them. It was true: I did. I'd always figured I'd make real friends when my true life began. So when I needed help, I was in trouble.

(This is an important lesson for you, one I wish I had learned earlier. Choosing friends is not an aspirational exercise. Your friends don't have to be as rich as you want to be, or even to share your dreams. You meet kind people, and you return their kindness. That's what friendship is. You take care of someone and they become yours. I have three close friends now: Martha, the town librarian; Paul, who works in the Photo Department at Walgreens and kayaks every evening; and Jayne. I'll tell you about her in a minute.)

When I picked up the receiver in Room 29, there was no dial tone. I decided to ask to use the phone at the front desk. I struggled to stand. In the mirror, my face was yellowish. I locked the door behind me and climbed slowly down the metal stairs that led to a dilapidated pool and the parking lot. Someone was cleaning the pool, and I stood and watched a young man skim leaves and algae from the water's surface. Noticing me, the young man nodded.

"Gotta try to better your surroundings," he said.

"That's true," I said.

As I made my way to the motel office, I saw a girl—maybe twelve, maybe younger—sitting in a broken chaise lounge near the parking lot. The girl was reading, her tangled blond hair stuck behind her ears, her freckled face angled downward. She was all bones in a T-shirt and shorts, her legs crossed underneath her, knees poking out. When I passed, the girl did not look up. She was reading *Forever*. . . . I loved *Forever*. . . . I loved everything by Judy Blume.

The office was closed and locked. I rested my head against the door. When I had gathered my strength, I started back to Room 29. A woman, a druggie, opened one of the doors on the ground floor.

The woman was in bad shape: alarmingly thin, her face droopy, wearing a dingy sundress and no shoes. Behind her, a man fastened his belt, pushed the woman aside, and exited. The woman sat down in the doorway, her privates exposed.

The woman's blank eyes reminded me of my mother's, though selling funnel cakes at Sea-O-Rama was a far cry from prostitution. Sadness fell across me—a wave, a shadow.

As I took the stairs up to my room, I saw the blond girl with the Judy Blume book approach the druggie. My stomach clenched. But the girl helped the woman up gently and led her into the motel room. Before shutting the door, the girl turned around and saw that I was staring. She lifted her chin and met my gaze. The girl's face was like an angel's.

This was Jayne.

10

Jayne

A mystery Jayne would ponder later, much later: what if you are in pain—terrible, ceaseless pain—but you are a mother? What do you do when your husband, once your love, comes home from Afghanistan and is haunted by whatever he'd seen, so haunted that he takes his father's hunting rifle and hunts himself, doing it in the barn where you once dreamed of raising baby goats? What do you do, after you've tried your best to make a life for your daughter, when a hurricane all but washes out your town, and an acquaintance tells you that if you crush your dead mother's pain pills and snort them up your nose you'll feel better—can you seek relief and remain a mother? Did the act of giving birth mean that you were no longer allowed to yearn for happiness for yourself—or, not even happiness, but the absence of sorrow?

Jayne remembers her father only vaguely. She was in kindergarten when he returned from a war she didn't understand. Everybody's father was gone; going away was the only job in town. Her father surprised her in the lunchroom, coming up behind her and tapping her on the shoulder. She thought it was a trick (which it was, actually) and refused to turn around. On the home video made by her mother, Jayne shakes her head and looks down at her sandwich. But then her father whispers in her ear. He says, "Hey, Noodle Girl."

Jayne knows then; she whirls into his arms and begins weeping. Her mother must have cried, too—the camera begins to shake. Jayne clutches her father tightly. He grins, looking up at the camera, at Jayne's mother, giving a thumbs-up. You can see Jayne's mother's name tattooed on his forearm. He is twenty-one.

There must have been some happy times, but her father came back to them volatile—you never knew what would upset him. Don't run up the goddamn stairs. Don't surprise me when I'm not expecting it. Don't you dare lock me out of my house. Don't tell me what to do. For the love of Christ, can you just, for one fucking second, be quiet?

Jayne was at school when he shot himself—by the time she came home, her mother had cleaned the barn and a neighbor had brought them dinner. It was fried chicken with Kraft macaroni and cheese. Her mother was probably more upset than she seemed, but what Jayne remembers from that night is a sense of relief. She and her mother ate dinner and watched TV.

Jayne didn't have a whole room upstairs, just a special "nook," as her mother called it, an alcove to the left of the stairs. Her father had built a bookcase lining the wall underneath a big window, then built a wooden bed for Jayne. It was made to last, said her dad. The night her father died, her mother sat with her in the nook. Jayne was warm in her mother's lap.

"Look at those stars," said her mother.

"Yes," whispered Jayne, looking out her window.

"One of those stars is your daddy. The brightest one."

Jayne pointed. "I see him."

"He's watching over us now," said Jayne's mother. "Everything's going to be OK now."

This was a comfort to Jayne, but in truth, she'd always loved her mother best. She curled in tight, put her thumb in her mouth, pulled a piece of her mother's hair to her cheek. She held on.

Jayne's mother got a job at the Dollar General, but then the Dollar General closed down. She got a job at the Silver Eagle, serving beer. Jayne came in after school and did her homework at the bar, loving her mother, loving the Shirley Temples her mother made her, each with three maraschino cherries.

Her mother began wearing shorter skirts, but at night, she still put on her quilted robe and let Jayne sit in her lap in the nook and watch the stars. "Which one is Daddy?" Jayne asked.

Sometimes, her mother would point, but sometimes, her mother said, "Oh, Noodle, if only I knew."

Even after she crushed her grandmother's pills and snorted them, Jayne's mother still belonged to Jayne. But when she came home from the Silver Eagle, she would go into the bathroom and come out dewy and euphoric, even her eyes calm. Jayne didn't mind making dinner. She'd eat fast so she could lie next to her mother in the nook, talking and talking, saying everything that came to mind, trying to believe that her mother was listening.

If it weren't for her grandmother's medicine, Jayne's mother would have left—Jayne knows this. It was only the false joy from the pills that allowed Jayne's mother to stay in the house on Chevron Avenue, to be immobile for hours as her daughter prattled on. The medicine helped her forget that she'd had dreams. The medicine quieted the voice that told her she was getting older, going nowhere, that this was her life and she hated it.

She hated every minute of it. Jayne knew, because on bad days her mother told her so. She hated making breakfast and seeing the broken burner that she couldn't afford to fix. She hated making school lunches and she hated making dinner. She hated the headaches and backaches and the cough she was starting to get from her Camel Lights. She hated that nobody loved her. (In these moods, she forgot about Jayne, who loved her so, terribly much.) She hated the Silver Eagle, serving drink after drink after drink. She hated Jayne, who trapped her with her needs, made her stay, canceled every route to a different life.

But everything changed with the needle. Jayne has thought it through back and forward and back again, and the needle is where it ends. The first time Jayne's mother opened her arm, exposing the pale, perfect skin inside her elbow, and allowed someone to use a syringe to puncture one of her healthy, blue veins, it was over. The medicine flowed into her bloodstream. Her head fell back. She was not a mother anymore.

11

Suzette

As she drove home from the hospital, Suzette thought idly about what Hyland might be making for dinner. He'd gone through a Chinese phase recently, and before that, it was all about the *sous vide* machine he'd bought at the culinary store on Montrose. My God, the boiled steaks were incredible! Most evenings, he'd finish up work by five, stop by the market, and begin preparing their dinner. By the time Suzette came home, worn out and ravenous, Hyland would be chopping and sautéing and the house would smell wonderful. Their cleaning lady, Nancy, bought fresh flowers for the dining room. She polished Hyland's family silver and set the table, every night, for two.

The rush-hour traffic slowed to a complete standstill. Through her tinted window, Suzette looked at a homeless couple camped out on the median with their dog. The man was youngish, with a scrawny frame and hair down to his ears. The woman might have been a teenager but looked forty, her face deeply lined. The dog was some kind of pit bull mix, shiny and frightening, panting under the Houston sun.

Suzette rummaged in her purse, but had no cash. The girl moved close, and Suzette fixed her gaze firmly on the car in front of her, an Oldsmobile with a POE ELEMENTARY SCHOOL bumper sticker. The girl hovered in Suzette's peripheral vision. Suzette might have (easily) become a person like this, slipping off the rails of society, though she'd never have gotten a dog if she couldn't care for it properly.

Suzette had grown up with a dog, a sweet, fluffy thing named William Blake (Blakesie). Suzette's father had been an English professor before his death; Suzette's mother had been his student. On the walls of their farmhouse, Suzette's mother had hung framed reproductions of Blake's creepy drawings of Heaven and Hell. Suzette hated those drawings. But she loved Blakesie, who slept with her at night. Suzette could still remember his wet fur smell, how warm he had been in her arms. No matter how things were at home, he was there. But every day she went to school, and left him unprotected.

Sitting on Westheimer, Suzette remembered how Blakesie, fifteen years old and hard of hearing, had followed Suzette on his last morning, never more than a few inches from her heels as she made her school lunch. It was May in upstate New York and the air was warm and completely alive with all the bugs and plants that had gone dormant during the endless winter.

She'd been annoyed with Blakesie, shoving him aside with her ankles, rushing around jamming her books in her knapsack. Her mother had been asleep. In the Houston traffic, Suzette was overcome with decades-old remorse. She should never have left Blakesie. She knew what her mother was capable of.

Suzette hit the garage door opener and parked next to Hyland's Volvo. She entered the kitchen to find it dark. On the counter was an empty box from Pizza Hut. "Hyland?" called Suzette.

He didn't answer.

In the living room, Suzette found a pair of socks and a Bud Light bottle. In the bedroom, her sleeping husband. Suzette yanked open the curtains, her hands shaking. (How many times had she entered her mother's dark, pungent bedroom?) "Get up!" she said. "This is no way to behave, Hyland. Jesus!"

Hyland rolled over, his eyes still shut.

"Everything is a mess!" said Suzette. "Where's Nancy?"

"Sent her home," said Hyland.

"This is no way . . ." said Suzette.

Hyland sat up, bleary-eyed. "We're never going to find her," he said.

"What about dinner?" said Suzette. "You didn't call. I didn't get anything."

"Dinner?" said Hyland.

"It's dark," said Suzette. "The whole house is dark! You left your socks . . . you left your pizza box . . ."

"Did you hear what I said? We're never going to find Dorrie," said Hyland. He looked at Suzette, and must have seen something in her expression. He made an effort to calm himself, sat up straighter. "I'm not your mother," said Hyland. "I'm just sad. I'm . . . overcome. What the hell are we going to do?"

Suzette shook her head. She felt a loosening, as if the fabric of her life were being pulled apart. "We need to make a plan," she said. She cleared her throat. "Dinner, let's make some dinner. We'll make a list. And then—"

"I'm sorry," said Hyland.

"Do you have a pen and paper?" said Suzette. "Let's find a pen and paper." She began to rummage in her bedside drawer.

"If I hadn't asked for more . . ." said Hyland.

Suzette faced him, eyes alight. She bit her lip to keep from saying the words, but they came out anyway. "That's right," she said.

"Fuck you," said Hyland, his voice loud. It was as if he'd been waiting for a reason to yell at Suzette, at someone. "Fuck you and your complete lack of emotions!"

Suzette shut the drawer, straightened, and walked out of the bedroom. She gathered her hands into fists, moving back through the house to the garage. Lack of emotions! She had spent her whole life learning how to observe, rather than be felled by, her emotions. It wasn't an easy skill, tearing yourself from yourself, remaining at a distance from your heart. Watching instead of feeling your deepest desires, keeping tabs on them, staying safe. If only she didn't have emotions at all—if *only*!

Suzette entered the garage, unlocked her car, and climbed inside. She would get takeout, is what she would do. She would put a good dinner on the table and they would go from there. She could already see the serene evening in her mind: chopsticks resting next to a list of methodical solutions. It was going to be fine. It was going to be fine.

Although she'd expected him to, Hyland didn't follow.

Suzette drove toward Try My Thai, planning on pad thai or a green curry with warm rice. But then she found herself veering the Lexus onto I-45 toward Galveston. Confronting Dorrie's mother, whom Suzette had never met, was not a smart plan of action. Suzette said aloud, "I'm going to turn back. Right here. I'm going to turn around and get Thai food." But she did not turn back, did not even put on her blinker. A ghost self rose within her, thrillingly stupid, a bit out of control. Suzette saw herself pounding on the door of a Galveston house, demanding the whereabouts of that idiotic child, Dorrie. She felt giddy, doing the dumb thing, for once.

Suzette placed a call to the Houston PD, getting Detective Whitlow on the line. "I was thinking that someone should go to Galveston and talk to Dorrie's mother," she said, her voice measured and calm.

"I went out there myself," said Whitlow. "Patsy Muscarello

says she hasn't got a clue. She's a religious old lady, works at Sea-O-Rama selling corn dogs. She seemed ashamed, to tell you the truth."

"Ashamed?" said Suzette.

"Yeah, it's the Catholic thing," said Whitlow. He sighed. "My wife's a Catholic. Everything's your fault, is what it comes down to. Ms. Muscarello's mother seemed embarrassed about her daughter. Told me she'd contact me herself if she heard from her. I'm sorry, Dr. Kendall, we've done about all we can."

"I'm going to go talk to her," said Suzette, pressing the accelerator of the Lexus, watching the odometer climb above the speed limit.

"Don't," said Whitlow. "I promise you, Dr. Kendall. You'll just make things messy. This Dorrie, she's flown off the handle, but she'll be back to roost, mark my words."

His statement was so asinine (*flown off the handle?*) that Suzette almost told him so. Instead, she inhaled deeply. "I'll just go home then," she said, watching her speed rise. She would be on Galveston Island by nine.

"Good idea," said Detective Whitlow. "You need anything, call me directly."

Suzette knew Whitlow was doing his best. But she wasn't convinced that his best was nearly enough. As always, Suzette was going to have to handle things herself.

12

Dorrie

When I left my room again, the girl and the druggie were nowhere to be seen, their door shut. Yet the resignation I had seen
in the girl's face reminded me of how trapped I had felt, when I
was too young to run away. Could the sweet girl possibly belong
to that wrecked woman?

I had run out of money. I was tired and hungry. I'm embarrassed to admit that I thought about driving back to Texas, just
giving up and returning to the fold. Your father and Suzette
would be fine parents, I knew: the mansion on Drexel Drive (I'd
driven by it—its front door was flanked with blazing sconces and
columns, like pictures I'd seen of the Acropolis!), the nursery
with the crib Hyland had picked out. He'd shown me pictures in
the Pottery Barn catalog. And the Kendalls had said I could visit
you. I'd suggested you could call me Aunt Dorrie, but Suzette
had laughed—a high, dismissive sound that said *no way*.

I considered it, my love, but I decided again that I couldn't live
without you. It wasn't possible and that was that. I couldn't even
imagine a life without you, not anymore.

Back in Room 29, I must have slept, because when I woke the sky was violet. I peeked anxiously outside the door and—seeing the coast was clear—stepped into the evening. The Astroturf was hot and prickly against my bare feet, the smell of tar and molten plastic somehow comforting. I peered down to the pool area. I saw the girl in the broken chair. She looked up.

Her face, so sad, glowing in the evening light. She turned back to her book, a new book. She must have finished *Forever . . .* I took a breath. "What are you reading?" I called.

She looked up again, startled. "Um," she said, looking at the cover as if she didn't know. "It's called *What Have You Lost?*"

I asked her if it was good.

"Yeah. It's poems," she said.

I asked her name.

She paused, put her finger in her book to save her spot, then called, "Jayne."

I said, "Hi, Jayne."

She shaded her eyes, peered up. "Hi," she said.

I wanted to keep talking to her, this sweet, miserable girl. But I couldn't think of one thing to say.

13

Jayne

At last, Jayne had found another mystery to solve, and the mystery was the woman in Room 29. Who was she? What was she doing at the Motel Claiborne? Was she hiding something—some treasure or a dead skeleton—in her room? Had she murdered someone? Was she going to?

Jayne couldn't tell if the woman in Room 29 was sick like her mom. Like Jayne's mom, the woman spent most of the day inside. Whenever she came out to buy a Sprite or peanut butter crackers from the vending machine, the woman looked scary. Her hair looked like small animals had made matted nests of her black curls. Her eyes looked freaky, too, like Jayne's mom's eyes when she didn't have enough medicine. But no boyfriends went into Room 29. From what Jayne could tell (hiding in the stairwell) the woman worked by herself. But whenever she came out of the room, she looked up and down the hallway, as if expecting to be busted. Jayne wrote this down. A good private investigator, she knew, paid attention to details.

By the entrance to the pool, there was a spot where a magnolia tree had pushed the fence aside. Between the fencing and the tree, Jayne made a special home for herself and spent evenings there when her mom was working. She had a pillow and a comforter someone had left outside their room. When it rained, she put her things inside the shed where the pipes led to the pool, to keep them dry. From her secret home, she could keep an eye on her mother and also on the parking lot.

Jayne kept track of all the people who entered and exited the Claiborne. It was 8:57 P.M. when the woman from Room 29 came outside. (Jayne checked her Casio watch, which someone had left on the bedside table of the room Jayne shared with her mom.) Jayne's mom had been working with a white boyfriend for twenty-three minutes. Night was the worst time at the motel. Everyone was out and about at this time, full of medicine and really loud and stupid. The early mornings were best, when everyone was asleep.

The woman walked back and forth on the second-floor landing. At 9:09, the woman went back inside Room 29 and shut the door behind her. Jayne wanted to go upstairs and visit the woman, but she knew that bad men were in the parking lot at night, so she stayed in her secret home.

14

Suzette

Galveston had been founded by pirates, Suzette knew, and then had been decimated by hurricanes again and again. Suzette liked the briny, near-fetid smell of the island and the way it kept on rebuilding—raising the grade of the entire city after the Great Storm of 1900, erecting new houses along the water every time the old ones were destroyed. In truth, she'd never considered what it must have been like to grow up in such a place: a playground for others, an island most visitors departed with a sunburn and a trinket, perhaps a hangover. There was a hospital and Galveston was a cruise ship mecca, but Suzette figured it was a place most kids left as soon as they were able.

Dorrie had told the Kendalls that her plan was to use the $35,000 to go to college. She'd been accepted at Rice, said Dorrie. What on earth had changed her mind? Suzette couldn't fathom what would make someone decide to turn down a fortune and go on the lam. Was Dorrie mentally ill?

A peeling sign welcomed Suzette to the island. She found her way to the Seawall, quiet in the deep evening, and trolled along slowly. Where was K½ Street? (She needed one of those GPS units.) How did the owners of all these homes support themselves on-island? (Suzette made a note to read up on the subject.) Should she stop for a rum drink? (No.) Finally, she located Patsy's rickety-looking bungalow.

In the rearview mirror, Suzette arranged her hair and applied lipstick. Hyland was probably worried sick about her, and good, thought Suzette. She climbed from the car, tucked her silk blouse in neatly, and walked to the door. One of those wooden wreaths Suzette had seen in the SkyMall catalog was affixed to the door. WELCOME TO OUR BLESSED HOME, said the wreath. Suzette looked for a bell but didn't find one, so she knocked.

After about five minutes, the door opened partway. A woman in a boxy bathrobe with a bun and granny glasses peered out. "Hello?"

"Mrs. Muscarello? I'm Suzette Kendall."

The woman paused. Even in the dim light, Suzette could see that she wasn't as old as she tried to make herself look. She was close to Suzette's age, in fact. "I see," said Patsy. "I'm sorry, I'm so sorry. But I don't think I can help you." She began to shut the door.

"Please!" said Suzette. "I don't know where to go. I . . . Please, Mrs. Muscarello. Please help me."

The woman looked at Suzette for a minute, and then she nodded. When she opened the door enough to permit entry, Suzette shocked both herself and Patsy Muscarello by leaning toward the woman, putting her arms around her. Patsy hesitated only briefly, then accepted Suzette's embrace and patted her on the back. "It's OK, dear," she said. "It's all going to be OK."

Suzette regained herself. "I'm sorry," she said.

"It's OK," said Patsy.

"I don't know what came over me," said Suzette, honestly. She cleared her throat. "I'm here to see if you have any idea . . . any thoughts at all . . . about where I can find your daughter?" At the word *daughter*, Suzette was seized with the desire to fall into Patsy Muscarello again, but she summoned herself and resisted.

"Would you like something to drink? Some tea?" said Patsy, leading Suzette into a small but tidy kitchen.

"Sure, thank you," said Suzette. She looked around the room, taking in the orange linoleum floor, particleboard cabinets, and olive-colored refrigerator. Suzette remembered hearing about an art exhibit in which an artist made a life-size replica of his 1971 childhood kitchen. Patsy's kitchen could be a museum piece, thought Suzette. At the haughty thought, she felt stronger, more like herself and less like the woman who had childishly begged for a warm embrace moments before.

"I appreciate your time," said Suzette. "We need to talk about a few things."

"I suppose," said Patsy. She put tea boxes and coffee tins in front of Suzette, and Suzette shook her head.

"Oh, have a cuppa," said Patsy.

Suzette shrugged, pointed to Sleepytime tea. Patsy Muscarello was like a mother from a movie. The housecoat! The International Coffee in various flavors! "So I have a few questions," said Suzette. "First of all, do you have any idea where Dorrie could have gone?"

Patsy looked deflated. "I don't. I have no idea. But I'll be honest with you, Dr. Kendall, I thought this whole idea was a bad one. By the time she told me about the whole . . ." Patsy made a disgusted face, then continued, "By the time she told me . . . your husband had already . . ."

Suzette put her head in her hands.

"I told Dorothy she'd regret this. She's so young, and she's fragile, more innocent than most girls."

"Look," said Suzette. "She met with the clinic psychologist. She was cleared."

"Cleared?" said Patsy angrily. "Whatever *that* means. And I'm sorry for you, you're old and you want a baby. I understand that. But Dorrie's just a child. Nobody asked me what I thought! Why didn't anybody ask *me*?" She banged a kettle down on the stove top. They sat in silence as the water heated to a boil. Patsy filled two mugs and brought them to the table, sinking into the chair opposite Suzette.

"She told us she wanted to help us," said Suzette. "She said she needed money for college, and she wanted to give us . . ." Suzette rubbed her eyes, remembering that the fertility clinic had told them that Dorrie's file wasn't complete, that she hadn't handed in all her papers. But Suzette and Hyland hadn't cared. They'd gone ahead anyway, choosing to believe what Dorrie told them, which was what they wanted to hear.

"You don't know one thing about her," said Patsy flatly. "Not one thing about her."

"But why did she want to be a surrogate?"

"I don't know," said Patsy. "Well, yes I do. She needed money."

Suzette nodded, realizing how much she had wanted to buy into the story of a saintly young woman who wanted to help the Kendalls out of kindness, who would trade a perfect baby for money and fade away.

"I love her, though," said Patsy, her eyes downcast. "I love her no matter what she does. I hope she knows that."

Suzette was motionless, dread filling her like a cold liquid. "Do you think she's . . . had a breakdown of some sort? Of a mental sort?"

"I don't know what," said Patsy. She stood, grabbed a framed photograph from the mantel, and shoved it into Suzette's hands. "Look!" said Patsy. "She's a good girl! She didn't mean to hurt anyone."

Suzette gazed at the picture of Dorrie, solemn in a white lace dress. She almost felt sorry for her. Scratch that, she *did* feel sorry for her. But then a new conception of Dorrie crept into Suzette's mind: a volatile girl who might have snapped, who might forever remain out of sight, existing only in their imaginations as the probable mother of Hyland's baby, someone who could be any-where, could be failing Hyland's child, or even *abusing* him or her. Life with this version of Dorrie would be more horrible than even Suzette could bear.

"I've got to find her," said Suzette. "Where could she be?"

"I have no idea," said Patsy. "I already said that. If I knew, I would tell you." She took Suzette's hand, squeezed it, and let go. "She'll come home," said Patsy. "This will all sort itself out. The baby will be fine."

"Do you really think so?" asked Suzette.

The phone on the counter rang, and Patsy leapt up to answer. "Hello? Hello?" she said. And then she turned away, but not be-fore Suzette saw her face change, almost melting with relief. Patsy's eyelids fluttered shut, her forehead relaxing as if being touched. Her shoulders caved inward.

"I'm sorry, she's not here," said Patsy, her voice soft. "This is a wrong number," she said gently. And then she put the phone down. She turned back to Suzette. "It was a wrong number," she said with an edge of defiance.

Suzette did not reply, staring at Patsy. There was a long mo-ment during which the only sound in the room was faint, tinny laughter from a nearby television.

"Well, it's late," said Patsy. She took Suzette's untouched tea, dumped it into the sink, and rinsed the mug. She opened the dish-washer door, pulled out the rack, and placed the mug upside down. "I don't think Sleepytime tea really does anything to make you sleep, do you?" she said. "You're a doctor, right? What's your professional opinion?"

Suzette didn't answer. Patsy hovered by the table. "Well, I'm going to go to bed," she said.

Suzette nodded and stood up. "May I use the bathroom?" she said. "Long drive back to Houston."

"Help yourself," said Patsy, indicating a powder room off the kitchen.

"Thank you," said Suzette. The bathroom was small with yellow carpeting and blue tiled walls. Three dolphin-shaped soaps rested in a ceramic container beside the sink. It was a shame to use one, but Suzette didn't see any other options. As she lathered the small animal, she stared at herself in the mirror. This was the home where Dorrie had grown up. It made Suzette uncomfortable to think about Dorrie as a person with a childhood home, with a childhood. It had been much easier not to think about her at all.

When Suzette came out of the bathroom, Patsy wasn't in the kitchen. Suzette lifted the phone receiver and hit *69, which Meg had told her about: apparently, when you hit these three buttons, the phone dialed the most recent caller.

Suzette heard Patsy's slippers whispering in her bedroom. The phone connected, rang once. Suzette gripped the doorjamb. She was short of breath, unmoored, standing in a stranger's kitchen on Galveston Island. Suzette bit her thumbnail, tore the edge clean off.

In the middle of the second ring, an answer. A brash voice, almost angry in Suzette's ear. "Motel Claiborne, New Orleans," said the man. "Motel Claiborne. Can I help you?"

15

Jayne

At 8:23 A.M., when the Front Office Man went upstairs to evict
the woman from Room 29, Jayne watched from her secret home.
The woman from Room 29 looked confused, clutching her backpack, but not sick. Her eyes were fully open and met Jayne's, unlike the half-lidded, dead eyes of the people who took medicine.
Jayne knew that her old house on Chevron Avenue was empty.
Jayne's mother had some money under the mattress. It seemed
that perhaps Jayne's prayers for a way out were being answered.

The first step was saying goodbye. Jayne went into her room
and watched her mother sleeping. Her mother's face had sores.
The skin was as rough as the paper bags she'd once packed Jayne's
lunches inside, back when Jayne went to school. She'd write
Jayne's name on the bag and draw a heart around it; it gave Jayne
a tiny thrill when she grabbed her lunch from the plastic bin each
day.

But now her mother's hair was lank, unwashed. Her lips were
bitten up and raw. Her arm was a landscape of scars. Jayne was
sorry. She was so sorry, but she knew that she didn't owe this

person anything, not anymore. If her mother was going to choose the medicine over Jayne, then Jayne could stop being her daughter. It was only fair. Jayne knew it was only fair. Still she cried as she ripped a page from her notebook.

She cried as she wrote, *I love you and I will always love you and do not worry I am going to be fine. From JAYNE*

Jayne took the blanket that was bunched at the foot of the bed and she drew it up, tucked it around this woman's shoulders. She laid her head next to this woman's head on the pillow and closed her eyes and remembered. Then Jayne kissed the woman, and said, "Goodbye."

Step Two was sliding her hand under the mattress and finding whatever bills lay there. Step Three was her escape.

16

Dorrie

I had struggled to wake when I heard a rough knock at my door. I sat up, nauseous and dizzy. The knocking continued. I stood, almost relieved that my sickly purgatory at the Motel Claiborne was over. I opened the door, and there was the man from the front office. He had let me make one phone call to Galveston, but even Patsy didn't want me anymore.

"Checkout's at eleven," he said. "Eleven yesterday."

I asked for a few minutes. He nodded. I dressed and put the motel soap and shampoo into my knapsack. I shuffled past him and climbed down the stairs. My throat was worse, my skin sweaty, my field of vision unnervingly blurry around the edges. I made it to the Mazda, got in, and locked the doors. I stared through the windshield, so tired I laid my head on the steering wheel and almost fell asleep.

It's hard to convey how lost I felt. Even though I knew I was out of options, I remained committed to keeping you. Making certain we would be together was the one thing that mattered to me, but it was also the one thing keeping me from going home.

Maybe you were my excuse to start a new life, I don't know. But I felt for the first time that I was doing something worthwhile, growing you (though you needed all of my energy, it seemed, and more food than I could afford or keep down). I knew you would love me, and I yearned for that love.

I jerked when a face appeared in the driver's-side window of my car. It was the girl who liked to read, Jayne. I shook my head—it was too late to make a friend at the Claiborne—but Jayne motioned for me to roll down the window.

"I saw you leave," she said. "I saw them kick you out. If you don't pay on time, that's what they do to you. I could have told you that."

I nodded, too worn out to engage.

"We used to have a house," said Jayne. Her eyes were pale hazel, her expression earnest.

"That's nice," I said.

"I can take you there," said Jayne. I remember thinking that someone needed to comb the knots from her sunlight-colored hair.

"I don't understand," I said.

"It was the hurricane," said Jayne. She looked over her shoulder, nervous (I guessed) that her mother would appear.

"What?"

"It's empty, my house," she said, insistently. "Since the hurricane."

"The hurricane?"

"We evacuated," said Jayne impatiently. "FEMA sent us here."

"I'm sorry, I don't . . ."

"Can you take me, too?" said Jayne. Her bangs were overgrown, and fell in front of her eyes. She shoved them aside. "I need to go home," she said. "I don't want to be here anymore. I have some money."

Again, I recognized something in her face—a recklessness born of desperation. She had her hand on the door handle.

"Please," she said. I had never heard a more anguished word.

Almost reflexively, I unlocked the car. Jayne got in the back and locked her door, as if someone might pursue her. She handed me a piece of paper with an address. "Don't you need to get anything?" I said. "A bag, clothes?"

"I need to go," she said. "I only need to go."

I started the ignition.

We drove out of the city in silence. The road shimmered with heat. My eyes welled with tears, and Jayne reached from the backseat and touched my hair. "It's going to be OK," she said. "I'll take care of you, and you'll take care of me."

I laughed, incredulous.

"That's how it goes," said Jayne, with an innocence that broke my heart clean through. "You belong with the one who takes care of you. Right?"

My instinct was to dismiss her. But in a deep place inside me (maybe it was your voice, already), I wanted to believe that this childish statement could be true.

17

Suzette

Suzette drove toward New Orleans. When she peered into the rearview mirror, she saw a stranger. A wreck. She looked scared.

This terror was familiar. Her childhood had been spent in an adrenaline-fueled haze of worried anticipation, trying to ward off problems before anyone found out about them. The farm where they lived was far from neighbors, which was both good and bad. On the good side, no one could hear Suzette's mother when she went on one of her tirades. On the bad side, they were on their own.

Suzette's mother and father had bought the farm together, hoping to make a life "off the grid." They pickled preserves, planted vegetables, and raised chickens. Pictures from that time made it look pretty nice, idyllic, even after Suzette was born.

Maybe her mother went crazy before her father died or maybe after. From Suzette's earliest memories, her mother was erratic and paranoid. There were plots against them. They were under siege. The phone had to be ripped from the wall. The radio was a two-way spying system.

Blakesie had wiretaps inside him that had to be cut out with a kitchen knife.

After a teacher took notice of Suzette's too-small shoes and too-long hair, visiting the farm to introduce herself and "just say hello," Suzette was no longer allowed to go to school. She wrote her own books. She studied *Where There Is No Doctor*, just in case.

There wasn't enough to eat. The chickens died. Suzette's mother was a city girl playing farmer's wife. She'd started with an inheritance, but eventually it ran out.

The last winter at the farm—Suzette's eighth—was the worst. Her mother told the social worker she was homeschooling Suzette, but unless ranting and raving counted as education, she was lying. Suzette sure did know a lot about government conspiracy theories, however, and also about the gold standard.

As Suzette drove east on I-10, reaching the end of Texas and crossing into Louisiana, she tried to force her brain back to the present. But memory kept washing over her. The last winter, she'd been so cold she got frostbite in three of her toes: they'd been amputated when she was finally taken away. Her mother by the hearth, her face like taffy in Suzette's fevered recollections. The way a neighbor had called the fire department after smelling smoke, and the fireman's reaction when he'd found Suzette, curled up in her room, in the midst of a house on fire, starved to almost gone. "Oh, Christ," he'd said. "Oh my God, there's a kid in here!" He'd turned back to Suzette. "It's going to be OK now, little one," he had said, gathering her up, but his expression—horrified, shocked—belied his words.

Suzette remembered looking out the back of the police car as they drove her away. There was her mother, in front of the flames, a heavy blanket over her shoulders. Her mother was screaming at Suzette. It was hard to understand her, but Suzette could just make it out: *I did all this for you.*

For a long time, the fire was all she remembered, her brain

mercifully blocking out the rest. But as the years passed, it all came back, piece by piece, as if the entirety at once would slay her. She'd grown up in adequate foster homes, gaining entrance to Columbia by sheer force of will. Her mother was committed to a mental hospital, paid for by Medicaid. When they'd saved enough, Hyland and Suzette moved her to a better facility. Suzette sent toffee at Christmas and a bouquet of flowers on her birthday.

Becoming a surgeon had given Suzette's life structure and meaning. A surgeon can never be lost. The best ones—the pioneers—were making up procedures as they went, creating what they needed to solve the problems in front of them, like Lewis and Clark on the Oregon Trail.

There was Michael DeBakey, who, as the famous story went, bought Dacron at the store when the clerk told him they were out of nylon. He then went home, grabbed his wife's sewing machine, and began making artificial arterial patches and tubes, which he went ahead and implanted in his patients. Successfully! (Though he and his colleagues rarely kept note of the failures, of course, so who knew?)

Suzette had just missed the golden age—the first artificial heart, the first bypass, the evolution of the heart-lung machine—still, every time she scrubbed in, she felt as if she were entering a new continent, armed and ready to conquer whatever lay ahead.

But now, away from the crises of patients whom she cared for but did not love, she was as fearful as she'd been as a child—and as unsure about how to fix things, how to make everything right.

Suzette drove into the city where her plan ended. To an outsider (and Suzette often thought this way—how "an outsider" might view her, though who this "outsider" was remained a mystery—most likely it was her mother, which was something Suzette should probably explore in psychotherapy, but wasn't going to), Suzette was a woman nearing forty who needed a shower. To an outsider, she was ineffectual, a catastrophe. In the hospital, she had status: she was listened to, and her instructions were the final word. But here, in a city she'd visited only a few times for medical conferences, all bets were off.

18

Dorrie

The landscape grew more washed-out, more desolate, the closer we came to the address the girl named Jayne had scrawled on the sheet of paper. In the backseat, she was silent, peering out the window with an apprehensive expression. At one point, I said, "Jayne?"

She didn't answer, didn't even look up. It was as if she'd decided that if she ignored my query, it would go away. But I felt as if I should try to draw her out, if only to make sense of what we were doing.

"At the motel . . . was that your mother?" I asked.

Jayne closed her eyes and pretended to be asleep. Fair enough. I was happy to be quiet, too. We were two battered ships in a storm, glad to have a port to steer toward. For the moment, it was enough.

Jayne's old neighborhood appeared to be completely abandoned. It felt like we were driving through a postapocalyptic film set: rusted-out cars, a child's empty jungle gym, sagging ranch houses with some front doors wide open. It was utterly silent, and I was unnerved. We had been the only car on the road for over half an hour.

Galveston, my childhood home, is such a vibrant place. Have you ever visited? There are festivals, the streets thronged with parades and loud music. At all hours, there are people out and about—filling up restaurants, claiming chairs on the beach, wandering the narrow streets in search of souvenirs. And there's the island light: the streetlamps in the historic district, the otherworldly glow of the Moody Gardens pyramids. At the beach, the sun glitters atop the waves all day, then turns them ruby red at sunset, luminous deep gray at night.

In contrast, the sky along the road to Jayne's house was completely flat, a cloudless tarp stretched above us. The hiss of my car wheels on deserted Chevron Avenue seemed a soundtrack of sadness.

Twenty-one Chevron Avenue was a small, bandage-colored home surrounded by a peeling picket fence. I parked the Mazda in a driveway riven with deep cracks. As soon as I turned off the car, a swampy heat descended, bringing with it a sewagey odor. I had read that some flooded homes had been completely submerged in filthy water for days. Eventually, the water had receded, leaving reeking structures to rot in the merciless Louisiana temperatures. Unless, of course, a penniless pregnant teenager and her skittish sidekick arrived to recolonize. And here we were.

Jayne was asleep (or feigning slumber) in the backseat. A bony cat guarding the walkway hissed, then sprang into the bushes. I watched Jayne for a moment, marveling at the courage it must have taken for her to approach me. I decided to let her enjoy as much sleep as possible before she was forced to confront the sight (and smell) of the place she'd once called home.

Leaving Jayne, I made my way to the front door. The knob was hot in my hand, but I could not turn it. I put my shoulder to the door and shoved: no luck. The house had been locked tight before it was abandoned. I made my way to the side of the house, where I found a window that had been shattered. I reached inside, unlatched the frame, and pushed the lower half up. Then, with some effort and squashing of an overgrown hedge, I scrambled inside the house.

The smell of mildew was dizzying. There was standing water in the room where I'd entered; it was the family room, judging from a waterlogged couch and wires snaking from the wall that must have once connected to a television. I was wearing flip-flops, and the water was warm and revolting around my ankles. There were cigarette butts in a bowl on a dingy coffee table, and crushed beer cans floating on the floor. Someone had eaten from Popeyes chicken and left behind the take-out bags, which were now teeming with roaches. I knew I couldn't blame my nausea on you, not this time. I ran into a small kitchen and stood, retching, above a dirty sink.

The refrigerator was open; there was no electricity. I was too afraid to open any of the drawers or cabinets. I tried to calm myself by figuring out what we would need to stay in this place. *Candles*, I thought. *Food that doesn't need cooking, instant coffee, bottled water.*

The carpeting on the final three steps of the staircase was still white—the water hadn't made it to the second floor. I found one bedroom with a queen bed that had been stripped of sheets and an alcove that must have once belonged to Jayne. We would need a battery-powered lantern and some sort of bedding.

A bookshelf held toys: wooden blocks, a plastic teaset, a moldering collection of stuffed animals. One elephant was not visibly damaged. I threw open the windows and sank to the floor. It was suffocatingly hot. I touched my stomach, thinking of you.

On top of the bookcase was a framed photo. I looked at the image: a mother and daughter at a table, a cupcake in front of them. The woman was a brunette with a full, sweet face. It must have been the woman I had seen at the motel, but it was impossible to reconcile the young mother in the picture with the junkie she had become.

The child, however, was clearly Jayne. In the photo, she gazed up at her mother, reaching out to touch her hair.

In that ruined, empty house, I began to weep. For one thing, I felt safe for the first time since I had fled Houston: no one was going to find me in this godforsaken place. But I also felt how fragile everything was, how one storm could take everything away, how being a mother was a job for life, not one that got easier, and not one you could abandon.

"I'm going to try," I told you. "I'm going to do my best for you, OK?"

My best wasn't enough, my love, but I didn't know that yet.

I looked up at the wall, at pictures someone had framed: a print from a Babar book, a child's drawing of a family—it was Jayne's drawing, I could see: a mother, a father, and a smiling girl in the middle labeled "J."

"You left me in the car," said a voice. I blinked and turned. "You said we had a deal," said Jayne, standing at the top of the staircase. "You said we had a deal and then you left me."

I stood. "I'm having a baby," I said.

Jayne pursed her lips. "How long?" she said.

"Six months."

"I'll help you," said Jayne resolutely. "I'll take care of you, and you'll take care of me, remember?"

The faith in Jayne's face! She'd been through hell: evacuation, the Motel Claiborne, watching her mother depart little by little. And yet, she believed in me—a complete stranger. Her hope made me want to prove her right, but I was pragmatic, and her plan was crazy. We were going to live in a decaying house together, until your birth? What would we eat? What would happen when you arrived?

I looked at the picture of Jayne and her mother. Could I become the person she needed me to be? Jayne stepped still closer. "You have a baby inside you," said Jayne, smiling. "Can I feel?"

I nodded. She put her warm cheek to my belly. Instinctively, I smoothed her hair with my fingers. And although none of my practical questions had been answered, everything seemed simple—and possible—in that moment. I ran my fingers through Jayne's tangled hair, and she leaned into me, and I held her up.

19

Suzette

New Orleans smelled rancid, like a bagged lunch left too long in the sun. There was a meaty quality to the air. Even in the morning, the heat felt stagnant, as if a breeze hadn't blown through the city in months. Once in a while, this overripe fragrance hovered at the edges of swampy Houston evenings, but in New Orleans, the stench seemed front and center. The streets steamed. Suzette's car bounced as she hit potholes. She remembered the motto: *New Orleans, the city that care forgot.*

As Suzette drove, she grew more and more anxious. Her entire existence, she saw now—the gated community, the same order at Starbucks, the precise time she returned home for dinner and her nightly two-point-five glasses of Pinot Noir—it was all designed to keep her from feeling this exact mixture of misery and ambiguity. Or, rather: this certain sense that there were awful things looming combined with a lack of knowledge about when, precisely, they would manifest themselves. How could you arm yourself for a threat without a name?

Suzette exited the highway. She passed a drive-through daiquiri shop, its neon sign listing flavors like Chocolate Kiss, the B. B. King, and Octane 190. Fortunately, the shop was open only between 4:00 and 11:00 P.M. As she drove by, slowing only briefly, Suzette sighed. She knew that both vodka and rum made her feel calmer (before making her feel sick, and then morose).

Tulane Avenue looked rough, even in the early morning. Two (or maybe three?) men (or maybe women?) were huddled in a scrum of blankets on the sidewalk in front of a deli ("Best Po-Boys in New Orleans!"). A prostitute (or perhaps just a regular woman having a lounge dressed in a short skirt and bra) leaned against a brick wall, seemingly asleep. Trash blew across the street. Suzette squinted, making out the MOTEL CLAIBORNE sign, a large blue sweep of metal with the name hand-painted on its side in white.

Suzette turned in to the parking lot, taking in the rows of motel doors, a walkway lining the upper floor. This place was even worse than she'd imagined. Suzette told herself that maybe, possibly—it wasn't impossible—she'd heard wrong when the man said "Motel Claiborne." But her stomach, pulsing with a dull ache, acknowledged the truth. Suzette got out of her car and locked it, the back of her neck prickling with the sense that she was being watched. There was a pool at the far end of the parking lot, and what seemed to be a trash dump to the right.

Suzette took a deep breath. What exactly was her strategy here? Just locate Dorrie, force her into the Lexus, and drive home? Here in Louisiana, the papers Dorrie had signed had no value. Suzette was sickeningly helpless. She strode toward the dented door marked OFFICE and pushed the bell.

Suzette crossed her arms and waited. Nothing happened, so she pushed the bell again, held it down until she heard someone fumbling with the lock. She put her hands on her hips. A stooped, balding man in pajamas appeared, and Suzette spoke. "My name is Dr. Suzette Kendall," she said authoritatively.

"You a cop?" said the man.

"No, but they'll be here momentarily if you don't tell me where I can find Dorothy Muscarello."

"I don't know what you're talking about," said the man, shaking his head. "Office opens at nine, ma'am."

"She's my height, with dark brown hair," said Suzette. "I know she's in this . . . establishment."

"Oh," said the man, nodding. "That one. She's gone."

"Gone?"

"She was here till today," said the man. "She didn't pay. Now she's gone."

"I'll need to see her room," said Suzette, trying to mask her frustration with a commanding tone.

The man snorted and shook his head. "There's someone in there," he said. "And I'm not waking *anybody*." He hesitated. "Was it her on the news?" he said.

Suzette nodded.

"Dammit," said the man. "Shoulda listened to Harlan. But I don't want no trouble, you know?"

"What?" said Suzette.

"Nothing, ma'am. Not a thing."

"What am I supposed to do now?" said Suzette.

The man paused. "Go home, lady," he said, shutting the office door and bolting the lock.

Suzette was silent, adrenaline making her heart thud fast in her chest. She listed her options in her mind. Driving home was an admission of defeat, and she couldn't bear to return to Hyland without any news. And if Suzette called the cops, she knew, they would tell her she had no claim to her baby, to the baby her husband had made!

Suzette walked slowly across the parking lot. This was a crack den, or a whorehouse, a shit show of a motel. If Dorrie could end up here, anything was possible. The desire to fix things and the impossibility of doing so twisted inside Suzette, making the pain in her gut worse. She paused by the pool entrance, gazing at the broken chairs and dirty water. Was it possible that the man had been lying? Could Dorrie still be here, behind one of the banged-up motel doors?

Someone had spray-painted LET GO AND LET GOD on the wall. Suzette stared at the words for a time. She'd seen the Alcoholics Anonymous slogan on bumper stickers before, but never writ so large. She shook her head. *Let go and let God* sounded fine and good, but when push came to shove, Suzette believed in action.

"Dorrie!" yelled Suzette, as loud as she was able. "Come out, goddamn you! Dorrie! Dorrie!"

A man wearing boxer shorts appeared on the upper-level walkway, his hand shading his eyes from daylight. "Keep it down!" he said.

"Where are you, Dorrie?" screamed Suzette. She ran to her car, unlocked it, and leaned on her horn. "Come out, goddamn you!" she cried, pushing the horn again and again. "Fuck you, Dorrie!" she yelled. "Fuck you, Dorrie!" It felt good to scream. It felt good to be out of control.

A woman in a dirty T-shirt opened a ground-floor door, squinting. "What's going on?" she said. She was little more than skin and bones, an addict toward the end of her run.

A sense of her own futility filled Suzette with fire. She leaned on her horn again. The man came down the stairs and approached her, pulling on pants. He looked jittery, strung out. "Hey," he said. "Come on now. You got to shut up now, lady. Calm down."

"Calm down?" said Suzette. She laughed, and the man's expression changed, growing angry. Suzette continued to laugh, emitting a barking sound, the sound of trapped sobs. Since the day she was taken from her mother's house, she had not cried, and she wasn't going to start now. In the distance, she heard a police siren. "Fuck you!" she said. *"Fuck you!"*

Suzette leaned into the car, blared the horn. When she re-emerged, she saw that the man was aiming a handgun at her. "Do you have a gun?" he yelled.

Suzette raised her arms in front of her, as if fending off an animal. "Do *I* have a gun?" she said.

The man fired. The sound was like a cannon. Even after he had turned and run, Suzette could hear the shot in her ears. Her leg bloomed with blood, and somehow she was sitting on the ground.

"Where's my daughter?" said the junkie in the T-shirt. She looked absolutely desperate. "Has anybody seen my daughter?" she said.

"I can't help you," said Suzette. She covered her face with her hands. She repeated, "I can't help you."

20

Dorrie

I suppose you'll learn this someday, or maybe you already know, but there are times when doing the right thing—the only thing, the *only good* thing—is impossible. It is not possible, and yet it must be done. Am I making any sense?

Jayne knew I was too big. But she had fed me so much—canned soup and milk and fresh apples from the Piggly Wiggly within walking distance. We used the money in her envelope, and then she begged for change. Somehow, she fed us both. I wondered if she stole, but I didn't ask. What would I do with this information?

It seems impossible that such a young girl was so capable, I know. But as Jayne told me of what she'd already survived, I came to understand that she was much older than her years. She'd been waiting for a way to start over, and she was going to make her new family work. When we realized we could not stay in her ruined house, she found a neighbor's house that had not been as damaged. Jayne found a way to turn the electricity back on. Again, I didn't ask. It was not an easy time.

When the pains came, she stayed beside me, three books about childbirth from the library open beside her. She'd studied the books for months, and had the phone number of a hospital on hand, in case things went wrong. (We'd discussed at length when we should call a hospital. I told her that I'd rather you be safe and taken from me than put at risk.)

It was hellish. I was twenty-one, technically a virgin. For twenty-eight hours, it went on, the pain like a drill. Jayne took notes about the moments you were born, and I will enclose them here:

- 3:26 p.m. Perineum bulging, placed my hand on introitus and perineum. D breathing well, told D to push gently to avoid tear.
- 3:35 p.m. Z head emerged, I kept pressure on Z head and chin.
- 3:38 p.m. Felt for cord behind ear, not found, THIS IS GOOD!!!
- 3:41 p.m. Amniotic fluid is clear, no need for suction.
- 3:43 p.m. Pressed down on head to encourage top shoulder to deliver.
- 3:44 p.m. I can see top armpit crease! Lifted up on Z's head to deliver bottom shoulder.
- 3:45 p.m. Z is here!!! Dried Baby Z, wrapped her in dry blankets. Discarded wet towels.
- 3:47 p.m. Oxygen ready, but Z's trunk is turning pink and her hands and feet, too.
- 4:04 p.m. Clamped cord 3 inches from abdomen and again 2 inches past that. Cut between clamps. Placed Z on D's chest with head lower than feet.
- 4:05 p.m. Gave traction on cord to assist in placental expulsion.
- 4:08 p.m. D says she is having contractions.

I don't know how Jayne remained calm, gripping my hand, forcing me to concentrate on my breathing, guiding your body into the world after your head finally, finally emerged.

You were so beautiful! I will never forget the first time I saw your face—eyes squeezed shut, mouth open in a protesting yowl—or the fierce way you latched on. From the first seconds, I knew you would survive. With the tools she'd bought and carefully sterilized, Jayne clamped and cut the cord that bound us.

"My baby," I said, holding you. You had my hair, thick and unruly. You had your father's fine nose. I was crying and laughing, overcome. "We did it," I said to Jayne.

"You did it," she said. We watched you suckle, still slick as a seal. We thought it was done.

But then the pains began again.

21

Suzette

On the baby's due date, after Suzette's leg had recovered and she had returned to work, she woke in the middle of the night. She knew their baby was in the world, knew it with complete certainty. And in the dark of the warm bedroom, she moved close to her husband. How could they go on, not knowing where the baby was, if the baby was all right, how the baby looked and smelled? It was not possible.

But what could she do?

Suzette closed her eyes and prayed, as she had once done while waiting for Camillo's heart to beat again. She whispered, *May you find the place where you belong.* Also, selfishly, *Please find your way to me.*

She was desperate. She was out of ideas. She was giving up. She was crying.

Maybe this was letting go and letting God.

22

Dorrie

For 603 days, you were mine. Do you remember?

23

Suzette

Deep in the winter evening, the bell rang. Hyland was cooking in the kitchen; the house was filled with the smell of browning butter. "Coming!" Suzette called, walking to the front door. Meg and her husband were due for dinner.

Suzette brought her eye to the peephole. Her breath caught when she saw Dorrie's mother, Patsy, in the lamplight. Patsy's face was mottled, as if she had been crying.

"Hyland!" Suzette cried, her voice high-pitched and shrill. "Hyland!" she screamed, fumbling with the lock. Hyland's footsteps coming quickly. Patsy, her cheeks wet, her expression morose. "Patsy?" said Suzette. "Are you all right, Patsy?"

"She told me, she said please don't look for her. You have to promise," Patsy said, her words tumbling over one another like stones in a waterfall.

"I don't understand," said Suzette, and then her gaze fell. A girl, not yet two, stood next to Patsy, gripping her leg. Her eyes were wide. Suzette could see a patchy rash on her cheeks and, yes, on her hands as well.

"Oh my God," said Suzette. "Is that . . . are you . . . ?" She knelt and gathered the girl in her arms without thinking. The girl was hot, too hot.

"Dorothy tried, but she couldn't do it," said Patsy. "She's real sick, there's something wrong. Dorothy tried, I'm telling you. But she . . ."

In Suzette's arms, the child made a jerky movement, then eased into Suzette's embrace. "Rheumatic fever," said Suzette, her body filling with fury. "How long has she been sick? We need to take her to the hospital right away, Patsy!"

"She'll sign whatever papers you need. But she needs to go on and live her life. You can't bother her ever again. You have to promise."

"What's happening?" said Hyland, appearing in the doorway. Suzette looked up, shook her head, too overcome to speak. She held on to the girl, who made the terrible jerking movement again. Rheumatic fever, which occurred when a strep infection went untreated, was almost unheard of in the United States. But Suzette's colleague Alberto had begun working in Africa with children whose hearts had been compromised by the disease; Suzette recognized the symptoms.

"She's real sick," said Patsy, dropping a duffel bag and backing down the front steps. "You need to take her to the hospital."

"This is Eloise?" said Hyland. "Oh my God, this is Eloise?"

"You can call her what you want," said Patsy. "It doesn't matter. It doesn't matter anymore."

"Hyland, get the car," said Suzette.

"I'm going," said Hyland, running back into the house toward the garage.

"Please leave Dorothy alone," said Patsy. "That's all I ask. She'll sign whatever papers you need."

Suzette looked up. The child must have been sick for months; the fact that Dorrie had waited so long to treat her made Suzette want to lash out. But she took a breath. "Tell Dorrie she's going to be OK," said Suzette. "I'll take care of her. I promise."

Patsy nodded. "I'll tell her," she said.

"I promise," said Suzette. She lifted the girl, so light, and held her close. "You're going to be OK," she whispered. "I've got you, baby. I'm never going to let you go."

Part Three

Fifteen years later

———————

1

Eloise

When I was sixteen, I decided to find my mother. My *real* mother, the one who was related to me by blood and not just by using her connections to get me into some fancy New England boarding school where she "sincerely hoped I would get my act together." Sincerely! You've got to love Suzette for her vocabulary. It's not a joke—she really said that, standing next to my dad (biological and literal) in the kitchen in Houston, Texas, a place where—true enough—I had pretty much messed things up.

"Your grades have been going steadily down," said Suzette. "Three Ds this semester, Eloise! And then the pills..." She stopped, then rubbed her eyes and said, "We sincerely hope you will get your act together."

Sometimes, when she was strict, I could see what she must be like in surgery, wielding knives or whatever. It was freaky. At home, she was usually in her pajamas doing bills. "We love you, sweetheart," she said. "This is a new chance. A fresh start."

A fresh start! I was living in an eighties after-school special.

"Dad," I said, leaning against the counter, making my eyes go soft. "You're sending me away?"

"Oh, Eloise," he said. He'd already told me that on the East Coast it was normal to go to boarding school. It was an opportunity. He'd gone to boarding school himself, though not the same one. Even being the daughter of the famous Dr. Suzette Kendall couldn't get me into a top-tier school. Not with three Ds.

My dad was enthused. The day before, he'd unearthed old photo albums, pointed to snaps of himself in a blazer and tie. Dorm pranks! Ice hockey! Late-night talks in bunk beds! Why, he'd once ridden a sled down the stairs in Pharis Hall!

I'd seen all the movies. I wasn't buying it.

But in the kitchen, when I was expecting more saccharine tales from his youth, my dad, instead, sighed and looked at Suzette. She blinked fast, which meant she was about to cry (again). "We both just think this is best," said my dad.

Something in me started to crack. And to stop the breaking, I ran into my room and shut the door tight. Out of desperation, I opened the medicine cabinet in my bathroom. Everybody always talked about feeling better after a beer, or schnapps, or Oxy. I'd never tried any of it.

But there in front of me was the bottle of cough syrup I'd used for last summer's cold. I remembered Fitz Hunter telling me about "robo-tripping." I unscrewed the cap and took a big sip. I held the viscous liquid in my mouth for a few seconds, daring myself to swallow. When I did, the medicine was fire in my throat. And then nothing. I stared at myself in the bathroom mirror. My fat nose. My limp hair. I had nice eyelashes, but that was it. First my best friend, Jenni, had ditched me to be popular, and now my parents were sending me away. I took another sip, and another. I was entirely alone in the world.

What about your real mother?

The thought came to me as if there was a person with my voice speaking in my ear. (Was this robo-tripping? Fitz had talked about things slowing down around him, and then seeing a parade of animated elephants.)

What *about* my real mother? The person whose genes I shared. I'd always wondered about her—what she looked like, if she missed me, if her voice would sound familiar. Was it being apart from her that made me feel so lost?

I would find her, that was what. If Jenni would rather be with all the pretty girls and football boys, and my dad and Suzette were packing me off, there was always my real mother. Maybe she'd want me. Maybe I could move in with her and start all over. I got into bed—it was true, I felt as if I was moving in slow motion—and was asleep within minutes.

A week later, I arrived at the Pringley School. Although it was still summer in Texas, in my new life it was autumn.

2

Suzette

When Suzette entered the Heart Centre, Africa's only free-of-charge hospital for cardiac surgery, Dr. Alberto Raid was kneeling in the hallway, talking to a young girl clad in a hospital gown. "Alberto," said Suzette, her happiness at seeing her former classmate canceling out her jet lag.

"Ah," said Alberto, "Suzette. *Bellissimo.*" He rose and embraced her. "I cannot thank you enough," he said, into her hair.

"I'm glad I could help," said Suzette.

"As am I," said Alberto. "Come, let me introduce you to Elizabeth."

The girl smiled shyly, hiding behind Alberto's leg. "She wants to go home, but we are not ready to say goodbye, not yet," said Alberto.

"You'll go back soon," said Suzette. "Who is your friend, there?"

The girl held out a stuffed bunny rabbit. "It's a princess bunny," she said.

"Ah," said Suzette. "I'm happy to meet you both."

• • •

Alberto (whom Suzette had kissed, only once and drunkenly, after their American Board of Thoracic Surgery In-Training Exam) had devoted his life to repairing pediatric hearts damaged by rheumatic heart disease. Eloise had been treated with antibiotics before her heart had been affected, but many children in developing countries were not. Even after Eloise's full recovery, Suzette had new appreciation for the Ross procedure, a complicated surgery during which a patient's diseased aortic valve was removed and then replaced with the patient's own pulmonary valve. Using a biological rather than an artificial valve had many advantages, most notably the fact that the patient would not have to take blood thinners, which made pregnancy inadvisable for female patients. In other words, giving a girl with a diseased heart a biological valve meant she might be able to grow up and have children of her own.

At Alberto's request, Suzette was planning to perform the first Ross procedure at the Heart Centre.

"Rheumatic heart disease—it is the disease of poor people!" Alberto cried that evening, as he made Suzette pasta in his spare apartment. "And it is the right of every person—rich or poor— every human, to have basic medical care."

Suzette blew on her tea. This was nothing she didn't already know and agree with. She wished it were morning—she was ready.

"These children's hearts, Suzette," said Alberto. "They are compromised. It is not good. Valves for shit. They are shit hearts."

"I've seen the echoes," said Suzette.

"I try to repair but—" He threw his hands up. "I have to replace."

Suzette nodded. Until now, Alberto had used only mechanical valves, which required the children to stay on anticoagulants for the rest of their lives. For the three little girls in the group (chosen because they were the most dire cases), Suzette's intervention would be life-changing. "I'll do my best," said Suzette.

"I know. I know you will—I still can't believe you are here!"

"Of course I'm here," said Suzette. "To tell you the truth, it was a good time to get the hell out of Dodge."

Alberto looked confused.

"I mean leave," said Suzette. "I needed a break from . . . my life."

"Tell me," said Alberto, who had made the mistake of placing his annual fundraising call to Suzette a few days after they had taken Eloise to boarding school. Suzette had cried on the flight home from Massachusetts, Eloise's angry voice ringing in her ears: *You don't want me! Nobody wants me! I wish I had never been born!*

Suzette knew that sending her daughter away was a mistake, and knew they couldn't keep her at home. Something had gone awry, and although she parsed it in her mind constantly, Suzette wasn't sure what she could have done differently. One night, when Eloise was three and still waking with night terrors, Suzette had collapsed in Hyland's arms, convinced she was doing something wrong: too much attention, not enough, the wrong nanny . . .

Hyland had held her and whispered the words she'd used as a mantra for the next thirteen years. "You just keep showing up," Hyland had said. "You hold her. You stay close. That's what it is."

"That's what it is?" said Suzette, who had never known a functional mother or father.

"That's what it is," Hyland said.

It sounded simple, but "staying close" in application was an unwieldy and perhaps impossible directive. To Suzette, being a mother felt like wrestling with a nuanced octopus of need and desire from the moment Eloise woke to her interminable yet precious "tuck-ins" every night.

Despite her demanding career, Suzette had been the Halloween party coordinator and the soccer "Snack Mom." (*Snack Mom! Just shoot me*, she'd thought, after volunteering for that one. And that was *before* she got the emails about peanut allergies and gluten and lactose intolerances! To top it off, all the kids groaned when she pulled out bags of apples and clementines, and Eloise called her the Mean Snack Witch.)

When Eloise was young, Suzette had even bought a minivan. A Honda Odyssey—the most ironic car name in the book: her only "odyssey" was to work, preschool pickup, and their house. The car so unnerved her that on the day Eloise aged out of her booster seat, Suzette left the van filled with Cheerios and juice boxes on a CarMax lot and drove away in a Volvo convertible, hitting ninety on the freeway before slowing down to a reasonable speed and returning home in time to relieve the Latvian nanny.

Years passed, and then the OxyContin. *OxyContin!* Prescribed three years earlier, after Hyland's root canal. It wasn't until Suzette discovered the pill bottle in Eloise's backpack that Eloise's increasingly volatile moods and slipping grades made sense. How could Suzette not have noticed that her daughter needed help? It was her job—her *most important* job—to protect Eloise as her mother had not protected Suzette. And she had failed. Suzette hated herself for this failure. She was ashamed. By the time Hyland brought up the idea of boarding school, Suzette was ready to cave in. What did she know about parenting—wasn't Eloise's slide into drugs spectacular proof that Suzette was a bad mother?

When Alberto called from Sudan, where the Heart Centre was located, Suzette was poised to make a change. "Staying close" sure as hell hadn't worked. Halfway through her conversation with Alberto, Suzette had brought up the idea of attempting the Ross procedure in Sudan. "If you think it's possible," she'd said.

Alberto had laughed. "I'll handle the red tape," he'd said. "Anything is possible, as you well know."

To be needed again in a straightforward way: it was worth the price of the last-minute plane ticket. Hyland had seemed utterly shocked when she told him, shaking his head and saying, "I always knew you were nuts."

"I found pills in Eloise's backpack," Suzette told Alberto, winding pasta around her fork.

"What pills?"

When she told him, Alberto's eyebrows shot up.

"I know," said Suzette. "And her grades are terrible. We've sent her to a strict boarding school in Massachusetts. In short, Alberto, I'm the worst mother in America."

Alberto exhaled and shook his head dramatically. "Suzette, you have always, always been so cruel to yourself."

"I guess," said Suzette. She preferred to think of it as holding herself to high standards.

"She's sixteen?" asked Alberto.

Suzette nodded.

"And you and Hyland, how are . . . things?"

"Fine. Good, I guess, considering the circumstances. We're doing our best."

"And your lovemaking?"

"Alberto! That is none of your business!" She punched his shoulder. Suzette and Hyland still turned to each other at night, still found solace in each other's bodies. She was lucky, she knew. But even her happiness with Hyland had a flip side—had Eloise felt left out, somehow? Had their union caused her unhappiness? Everything unraveled in the same direction: *why* was Eloise so sad?

"I was going to offer my services . . ." said Alberto.

"Thank you, that won't be necessary," said Suzette, laughing. It felt wonderful to be with Alberto, who had known her for so long. (And who still flirted with her.)

"At least you have a child," said Alberto, who had known both love and lust, but never fatherhood.

"All the kids who come here sick, who you send home well . . ." said Suzette.

"It's not the same," said Alberto.

Suzette nodded. He was right.

"OK," she said, changing the subject. "Tell me about my patient."

Alberto moved the patient folder to the center of the table. "Her name is Angel," he said. "I should not have a favorite, but Angel is my favorite."

3

Hyland

For years, Hyland dreamed of his mother. He woke in a cold sweat, feeling like an idiot. Really? Really, after all these years, even now that he was a fifty-five-year-old man, a productive adult member of society, really, still, dreams of being held close, looking up at his mother?

She had been gorgeous, Hyland's mother, with mahogany hair (it brushed against his face when he sat in her lap) and eyes the greenish, muddy color of Roxbury Falls, where they swam on summer weekends. She was wonderful, he loved her so much, she was dead. But at some point, couldn't his unconscious brain move on? He never dreamed of Suzette—she was too all-consuming in his waking hours to be relegated to the sepia-toned filmstrips of dreams.

What was it he longed for? Because he woke filled with an aching need, one he couldn't honestly place, except to think, *I want my mommy.* He'd lie in bed, his breath short. He touched his wife between her shoulder blades, put his face in the warm, open place underneath her jawbone. He breathed in the smell of her, impossible to describe, yet a scent that made him calmer.

I want my mommy, he thought.

He remembered his father only occasionally. His father had been a shadow presence, distant and irritable. He'd spent his evenings sequestered in their wood-paneled den, smoking and watching TV. Even a knock on the door to tell him that dinner was ready would be met with an exasperated sigh, one that said, "Jesus, what do you want *now?*"

He'd wanted a real man for a father, but that was old news. Once in a while, before he was able to quit his job, Hyland had had a client who reminded him of his father—some rich guy with absolutely no idea that the monstrosity he was forcing Hyland to design would bring him none of the joy he was hoping for. The Versailles-like entrance hall, the cantilevered awnings over the pool bar, et cetera: a stage set for a midlife crisis. It had been Hyland's job to nod and murmur appreciatively, to bring these people's fevered visions to fruition.

But that was long ago. On the day Suzette was named chief resident, she sent him a text: *This is your last day at Glencoe & Associates. Congratulations, my love—and thank you. XXOO and XXX later, Your Happy Wife.* He sat at his desk for a moment, letting the news wash over him, taking a final look at the view from his office. And then he picked up Eloise's fourth-grade school picture and his favorite coffee mug, went to Frank's office, and said (with relish), "Frank? The time has come. I quit."

He ordered a prefab, modern shed on his way home that very day. As soon as it was set up in the backyard, he began spending mornings inside with his sketchbook. He brought out his easel, purchased paint and brushes. After school, Eloise joined him. They shared a plate of fruit or cookies, listened to their carefully cultivated playlist. Hyland helped Eloise with her homework (when he could—algebra was harder than he remembered). She was a moody girl, often reticent. When he hugged her, she didn't always hug back. Small things bothered her deeply—she worried about animals being mistreated at the zoo, or an old lady she saw at the bus stop with a vacant stare. She wasn't much for joking around. Hyland grew to appreciate their silent companionship.

Before Eloise went off the rails, Hyland had been planning a trip to Paris. He wanted to take his family to the Musée de l'Orangerie, to stand between his daughter and his wife and gaze at *Water Lilies*. The first time he'd encountered Monet's murals (it was a rainy day), he must have stood before them for an hour. A cliché? Fine, so be it. He appreciated beauty. It made him feel closer to his mother. Yes, always back to her.

Once, coming downstairs and watching Eloise climb into her mother's lap to watch some god-awful television show, he was struck dumb with yearning, jealous of his own daughter.

But Hyland had been through years of analysis. He went back to the room he shared with Suzette, sat on the edge of their bed, pulled his knees to his chest, and allowed himself a short (and fairly manly) cry. He missed what he'd had, and what would never be again. That was just the way it was. Oh, his mother. Her glossy hair.

It wasn't until Eloise was older that Hyland started seeing a boy in his dreams. Hyland would be stuck in a castle fortress, or learning how to fly, and a boy would arrive, seemingly an ally.

Once, Hyland had a dream about being a bartender (he'd bartended, badly, on Martha's Vineyard one summer) in a bar full of his worst architectural clients, all of them ordering fancy drinks he couldn't remember how to make. Suddenly, the boy had shown up beside him, cheerfully grabbing bottles and flipping them around like Tom Cruise in the movie *Cocktail*.

(When Hyland mentioned the dream to his analyst, his analyst pursed his lips. *Latent gay tendencies*, Hyland had imagined him jotting down in his secret little pad. *Wants to "mix drinks" with Tom Cruise.* But it wasn't sexual, truly. It was more a feeling like "Oh, thank God. I'm not alone in this.")

At least it wasn't his mother anymore. The boy showed up infrequently, and unlike everyone else in Hyland's life (and dream life), he didn't seem to need anything from Hyland. The boy just appeared in the spaceship, tunnel, or weird old house-that-was kind-of-like-his-boarding-school-dorm and joined in whatever hunt, escape, or challenge was going on. He looked at Hyland with affection. Even, sometimes, with pride.

One night, Hyland dreamed of sitting at the edge of a lonely pond in winter. It was bone-chillingly cold. Hyland was exiled from somewhere or something, this wasn't made clear. He tried to find a way out of the woods, but kept circling back to the frozen pond. He felt the acidic beginnings of despair. He sat on a log. It was silent.

The boy appeared. He carried a hockey bag and two sticks. This boy, so carefree, his face ruddy. He tossed a puck onto the ice.

Hyland looked down to see that he was already wearing skates.

4

Eloise

In the dining hall, about a week into my new, boarding-school life, a girl named Raphael (seriously; she was Italian, from Italy) asked me about my parents. I related the narrative I'd been given: a mother with a history of mental illness who dreamed of a non-crazy baby; a virile father; a kind surrogate who vanished as soon as I was born.

"So you've never met your real mother?" said Raphael.

"I've never met my *surrogate* mother, no," I said.

"Oh my God," said Muffy (I know; she was from Connecticut), a skinny blonde who was eating her peas one by one.

"I wonder if she looks like you," said Muffy's identical twin sister, Trina (also anorexic).

"Because you don't look *anything* like your mom," said Muffy.

"Your mom's really pretty," said Raphael. "I saw her on Orientation Day. I like her red hair."

"What are you saying?" I joked, trying to be brave.

"Oh my God, nothing! You're pretty too! Just . . . in a different way," said Muffy.

"Don't get so sensitive," said Trina.

I left dinner with a bad feeling in my stomach, and not just from the turkey loaf. My therapist had taught me to call the voice in my head the Tape Recorder of Doom when it said things like *You are ugly, no one loves you, your mother and father might die tonight.* And I tried. But sometimes, it didn't feel like a tape recorder at all. It felt like what was real. Cough syrup seemed to be helping.

That night, when the syrup made me less terrified and more sleepy, even languid (great word), I started thinking, again, about how I could locate my real mom. I didn't even know her name. I started thinking about who, besides my parents, might know something.

I came up with my crazy grandmother, who was another person I'd never met. Another road Suzette said it was "best not to go down."

I knew a few things about my sole surviving grandmother:

1. Her name was Carolyn Greene.
2. She lived (not by choice) in a mental institution called Bellevue. It was hard to find info about Bellevue—it had been renamed NYC Health + Hospitals/Bellevue—but I knew the address: 462 First Avenue, New York, NY.
3. Carolyn's disease was called bipolar disorder with psychosis, which meant she thought everyone was out to get her. This is not the same as hearing the Tape Recorder of Doom, but much, much worse. The Tape Recorder of Doom is a normal thing for a young girl to hear, and is otherwise known as being anxious, so stop worrying, Dr. Kendall, your daughter is fine, not completely nuts like your mom. (An aside: maybe Dr. Kendall could use some new meds, as well?)
4. I was never brought to visit my crazy grandmother because she had threatened to come to Houston and burn down our house. She believed my dad was evil/the devil/part of a gov-

ernment conspiracy to ruin her/the universe as we knew it. My parents agreed that having her in my life was a bad idea. (They agreed about pretty much everything, leaving me feeling like the perpetual third wheel.)

As if it were fate, during Dinner Announcements the next night, Ms. Phillips announced a field trip later in the semester to the Museum of Natural History in New York City. I was the first one to sign up. After I signed up, I went to the auditorium, where they were holding tryouts for the Pringley Girls a cappella group. I watched the tryouts, wondering if I could find the courage to give it a shot. If I went for it, I decided, I would sing an Ella Fitzgerald song—"Love for Sale" or "They Can't Take That Away from Me." (I sang Ella in the shower, and to be honest, I was kind of good.)

In a red velvet chair, watching other girls with more courage than me but not necessarily more talent, I mused about my real mother. Who was she? Did she hear the Tape Recorder of Doom? Did she have black hair like me, just a bit curly—and brows that needed serious tweezing? Did she also love to swim? Was she a good singer? How could she give me up—just hand me to the Kendalls and disappear? Was she dead?

I was pretty sure she wasn't dead. I would know. I just knew I would know.

Somehow, and without any Robitussin, I walked to the stage and waited in line. When it was my turn, I stepped into the light. "Hi," I said. "Um, I'm going to sing 'The Nearness of You.' It's an old Ella Fitzgerald song."

"OK," said a tall brunette sitting in the front row with a clipboard. "Let's hear it."

I took a deep breath. I closed my eyes and thought about being held in someone's arms, close and warm. Safe. The words spilled out—rich, deep, lovely.

When I finished, there was the deadest silence I have ever experienced. I narrowed my eyes to try to see what the brunette thought. She was looking at me with a half smile on her face. "Excellent," she said, nodding.

I smiled.

That night, I did not drink any cough syrup. This seemed like a significant step for me. I thought about my real mother as I fell asleep. She must have cradled me as a baby—at least once. While I was singing, the feeling of being held wasn't like a dream. It was like a memory.

5

Suzette

After a fitful night in Alberto's bed (he insisted he sleep on the couch) and two of his strong espressos, Suzette arrived at the hospital. A television crew waited in the hallway. Suzette held up her hand as they approached and turned to Alberto. "Please, Suzette," he said. "Any publicity is good for us."

"We'd appreciate a quick word, Dr. Kendall," said a woman in a chic, cream-colored suit.

Suzette sighed but acquiesced. "You could have told me to wear lipstick," she said, sotto voce, to Alberto.

"Yours is a natural beauty," he replied.

"Flattery will get you everywhere," said Suzette. "All right, let's do this."

The newscaster lifted her microphone. "Tomorrow morning, Dr. Suzette Kendall will perform a very complicated, very long heart surgery here at the Heart Centre," she said to the camera. "Dr. Kendall, can you explain the Ross procedure?"

"Of course," said Suzette. She explained the operation as simply as she was able, but the woman cut her off.

"That sounds very dangerous," she said, her brow creasing.

"It *is* heart surgery," said Suzette.

"Why would you operate in such an involved manner, when you could just replace the valve with one made of plastic?"

"There are many advantages for a biological valve," said Suzette. "But most importantly, an artificial valve requires the patient to take blood thinners for the rest of their life."

"Yes? And the problem?" said the reporter, her voice light but her question rude.

"Well, for one thing, a patient shouldn't be pregnant while on anticoagulants."

The reporter nodded, moving on. "What is the success rate?" she asked.

"For the procedure worldwide, I'm not sure. But I have never lost a patient during the procedure."

"Never?"

Alberto stepped in front of Suzette. "Dr. Kendall is one of the most accomplished surgeons in the world," he said. "And now she must get to work."

"We will be waiting to hear the news of the surgery," said the newscaster. Suzette smiled, deciding to ignore the note of menace in her tone.

The Rwandan children looked small and scared in their halogen-lit rooms. To a one, they were gravely ill, their valves severely compromised. Without heart surgery, they would die before long. Even *with* surgery, Alberto had told Suzette, their chances weren't great.

Angel was a small girl with close-cropped hair. Alberto introduced Suzette, and Angel said, "I am very pleased to meet you."

Suzette grinned at her formal tone. "I'm glad I can help," she said. "Do you have any questions for me, Angel?"

"You will make me well?" said Angel.

"I'm going to try my best," said Suzette.

"And I can still have a baby?" said Angel.

"I hope so," said Suzette. "But you're only eleven years old. You don't need to worry."

"Do you have a baby?" said the girl.

"I do. I have a daughter. But actually, another woman was pregnant, not me. She gave the baby to me." Suzette smiled, trying to be positive.

Angel narrowed her eyes. Her eyelashes were lush against her ashen skin. Her arms were stick-thin. "The mother, she died?" she asked.

"No," said Suzette. "It was . . . a job for her."

Angel looked dismayed. "Oh, no," she said. "That's bad."

"No—it was . . . it was a complicated arrangement."

Angel crossed her bony arms and stared at Suzette.

"The point is that there are many ways to become a mother," said Suzette. When Angel turned her head away, Suzette said gently, "Let's make you well, OK?"

Angel turned back, nodded slowly. "Yes. It's my heart," she said, bringing her small hand to her chest. "My heart is sick," she said.

Suzette placed her hand atop Angel's and they sat quietly for a time.

Suzette scrubbed in and stood next to Alberto in the OR. The plan was for her to observe for a day. On the table, a nine-year-old boy was prepped for surgery. Suzette watched the fragile expanse of skin over his rib cage rise and fall. His lips were parted beneath the oxygen mask.

"You are here for how long?" asked Mugwaneza Cyilima, the doctor who had accompanied the children to the world-class hospital, which had been built in Sudan to serve the nine neighboring countries.

"I don't know," said Suzette. She had told Hyland it would be a week, but now that she was here, Suzette didn't ever want to leave.

"I am here for three days only," said Mugwaneza. "I will watch the surgeries, then go home. There are many others..." He trailed off, opening his hands to convey multitudes.

Suzette nodded. She had been told that Mugwaneza was one of two pediatric cardiologists in his entire country.

"The children will stay for six weeks at least," said Gwyneth, a nurse. "They get so homesick without their parents, but we must make sure they've recovered."

Suzette had little patience for pleasantries in the OR. She turned to Alberto. "Let's begin," she said. He nodded. The staff seemed reassured by her brusque demeanor. Alberto readied the scalpel.

When the boy's chest was open, Alberto cut a glance to Suzette. The left atrium was huge, the boy's heart so enlarged it was practically beating out of his chest. Suzette had never seen a heart so diseased, except in training videos. She was overcome with sadness. If Eloise had not been treated, her fever could have led to this.

Suzette knew what Alberto's look meant—he could not repair the valve, and would have to replace it. "Start bypass," said Alberto.

"Bypass on," said the nurse.

Suzette listened to the robotic symphony sustaining life as the boy's heart, slowly, stopped. Gwyneth readied the tools. Alberto breathed in. He looked again at Suzette, raised an eyebrow. "Tomorrow, it is you," he said.

"I'm ready," said Suzette.

That evening, after Alberto had completed five successful surgeries, Suzette made dinner—noodles with butter and the desiccated contents of a jar labeled "Italianate Blend." Thanks to Hyland's skills, she had never really learned to cook.

Juggling motherhood and work during Eloise's earliest years had been torture: Suzette would wake with a sense of dread, scrambling to figure out how she'd get through the day—the endless to-do lists, Hyland's hatred of his job, the nannies and their myriad needs. Suzette loathed saying goodbye to Eloise. "Mommy!" Eloise would wail, reaching out. And after a while— even worse—Eloise stopped caring when Suzette left, simply turning toward (and gazing lovingly at) the nanny. Suzette almost quit her job a thousand times, but something in her could not do it.

Suzette savored their weekends together as a family: they went to museums, zoos, Asian markets, thrift stores. They napped together in Hyland and Suzette's big bed, then woke and ate apples with peanut butter. On Eloise's first day of kindergarten, Suzette had felt bereft. Luckily, Meg—who knew the feeling well— spirited Suzette off to Perfection Nails, where they toasted Eloise with plastic glasses of champagne and gave their pedicurists ridiculous tips. (Lenny was long gone—to Las Vegas, he had told them, where he planned to open his own salon and remain "single and out and about.")

"To Eloise," Meg had said.

Tears had leaked from Suzette's eyes. "To Eloise," she'd said. "I love her so much."

"It's a bitch, that's for sure," Meg had said, summing up the situation perfectly, as usual.

The years had passed so quickly, as the greeting cards said they would. And while the daily chores often seemed thankless, there were transcendent moments almost every day: watching Eloise and Hyland dissolve into laughter watching *The Jerk*; tasting a pizza Hyland and Eloise had made together; playing Holiday Charades on Christmas. It wasn't until Eloise was fourteen that she'd stopped wanting to spend her weekends with her parents. In a matter of weeks, it seemed, she became a stranger. Suzette missed the Eloise who had been her best friend, who had wanted to spend the summer watching classic movies and trying new restaurants with her mom.

"Suzette, this spaghetti is delicious," said Alberto. "But are you with me? You seem a million miles away."

"Sorry," said Suzette. "Here, don't forget to squeeze lemon on top."

"Perfect," said Alberto.

After dinner, they stayed at the table, sharing a pot of mint tea. "You think it is possible, the Ross procedure in this OR?" Alberto asked, rubbing his eyes, stubbing out his cigarette and lighting another.

"Yes," said Suzette. "It's possible."

"We'll see," said Alberto. "It remains to be seen." He took her hand, but instinctively she pulled away. They had known each other for a long time—neither needed to say a word.

6

Eloise

As it turned out, New York City was nothing like Houston. Having been to only one city—my city—I thought they were all similar: shiny, busy, filled with swanky cars and people with impressive hairdos. God, I was wrong. As soon as the Pringley School bus dropped us off in front of the Museum of Natural History, I could tell Manhattan was different. The air literally smelled like chestnuts roasting on an open fire. People didn't smile. Their clothes were black and gray. They seemed much more important than the people at home.

After I hadn't even gotten a callback for the Pringley Girls, things had gone downhill. It was easier to guzzle Robitussin in boarding school than at home. Nobody was checking my grocery bags or my wastebasket. You could get other stuff, too. One of my new, druggie friends had even provided me with the number of her NYC dealer. I was sticking to cough syrup, but it seemed like I needed more every night to shut up the Tape Recorder of Doom and fall asleep, which was worrisome.

My plan was straightforward: board the bus from Pringley to

the Museum of Natural History, escape the school group, ride the subway to my grandmother's mental hospital, pump her for my real mother's details, then embark on my Journey of a Lifetime. (Yes, I had capitalized it in my head.) I had a credit card for emergencies, and obviously figuring out who I really *was*, where I came from . . . if my real mother could explain me to myself, maybe help me feel less raw and lonely . . . well, if a Journey of a Lifetime isn't an emergency, then what is?

At my old high school and now at Pringley, I tried to fit in. I missed being in elementary school, back when Jenni and I had each other and didn't really care about everyone else. I tried not to think about the day I stood in the cafeteria with my tray of pizza scanning the room, looking for Jenni, with whom I'd eaten lunch every day since kindergarten. When I saw the back of Jenni's blond head at the popular girls' table, I felt my stomach drop. I approached, and Mindi glanced up and then back down at her salad. She whispered something, and Mandi and Joni giggled. Jenni turned around and looked at me. "Hi," I said.

"Hi," said Jenni.

"Is there . . . room for me?" I asked.

Jenni looked at Mindi, who shook her head. Jenni's face was blank. She could have stood up for me, but she did not. I nodded, made a face like it was fine, and walked away. I didn't cry until I was in the girls' bathroom.

I never spoke to Jenni again. She dropped me cleanly and without malice. She'd been picked, and I had not.

At Pringley, I watched the groups of kids laughing together like a scientist: how could you be so comfortable? How did you know the right way to respond to perplexing comments? For example, one day I decided I needed to leave my room and try to socialize. I walked into the common room of my dorm and a cute boy named Wesley said, "Oh, look who's here! It's Eloise! We're *so glad* you're here, Eloise." The way he said "so glad" made it sound as if he were making fun of the words. As if he wasn't glad at all. I put my hands on my hips. It had taken me about an hour to put together my outfit of low-rise jeans and a halter top.

Later, Muffy told me I had to "give it right back" to people like Wesley. What did this mean? How would this work? None of it made sense to me, and when the group of boys around Wesley laughed (at me? It sure seemed like it), I felt the usual sinking sadness. I turned and went back to my room, as if I didn't care. But I did care.

I guess I thought that if I found my real mother, and she was like me, maybe she'd help me sort it all out. She might know how to respond to people like Wesley. If I asked my dad, I knew he'd say, "Ignore it." (I tried. It still hurt.) If I asked my mom, she'd say guys like Wesley were losers who'd never amount to anything after college. But that knowledge didn't help in the short term. It didn't make any difference at all. I wanted Wesley (and boys like Wesley) to like me. I wanted to belong. I wanted to be like Wesley myself, but I didn't know how.

The Museum of Natural History was an easy place to disappear. I told Ms. Phillips I had to use the bathroom, actually *did* use the bathroom, and then I walked underneath the insanely awesome giant whale and took an elevator to the basement. There was a staircase leading to gleaming metal doors—the entrance to the New York City subway system. I pushed the doors open, awkwardly mashed a few bills under a glass partition, grabbed a MetroCard, and I was on my way. It took me a few slides of the card through the jobbie on top of the turnstile, but eventually I found myself on the platform. I could go anywhere. I shivered in anticipation.

I'd already planned my route to my grandmother's mental

hospital, which was located way downtown. I'd memorized the directions, because anyone who's ever run away knows you need to turn off your phone and its Big Brother tracking system. As far as Big Brother knew, I was still in the ladies' room at the museum, perched on top of a toilet.

I had never been on a subway, but I tried to look nonchalant as the train approached. It was ridiculously loud, but nobody flinched. Also, nobody looked at each other. It was weird, like we were all robots who didn't bat an eyelid when we heard deafening noises or happened to be standing like inches from another person's face. I thought: *New York is not for me.*

I was also feeling nauseous from the cough syrup party I'd had with myself the night before. After maybe six or seven sips, I'd found myself in my dorm bathroom wearing an oversize Pringley T-shirt with no pants, looking at myself in the mirror and saying, "What are you searching for? Is it inside yourself?" out loud. That was the last thing I remembered before my phone started making the obnoxious alarm sounds that heralded another Massachusetts morning.

I stood on the platform. My train braked to a stop. The doors wheezed open and a tsunami of humanity poured out. I scrambled onto the train, grabbing one of the metal bars that hung from the ceiling. I had only the hundred dollars cash my mother had sent the week before for "fun money" (along with a dopey card of a dog with a tear rolling down its cheek, captioned "I Doggone Miss You." If she missed me so much, why did she send me away?). Still, I thought I might take taxis from now on. The whole subway experience was bringing me down.

I had to change trains at Times Square, which I almost went up and saw in real life—New Year's Rockin' Eve and all—but then realized I'd have to pay to get back on the train, so I just followed endless passageways past people singing and playing drums and apparently sleeping. Again, I had that "human in a robot world" feeling, as everyone's gaze just slid over me. Nobody even paused to check out the posters for Broadway shows and nose jobs. I saw a man kneeling next to his son in a stroller, feeding the boy frozen yogurt right there in a subway tunnel.

Something about that man kneeling made me think of Suzette, which made me sad. She loved me so, so much that it was burdensome to think about. She was the one who'd quizzed me on my multiplication tables for months. She was the one who stuck love notes in my lunch bag. She came to me when she found the pills in my backpack. "Why, honey?" she asked me. "Why?" I'd almost told her the truth: Joni had told me there would be a party at her house after school, and that if I brought beer or drugs, I could come. I'd skipped last period, walked home, and rifled through our liquor and medicine cabinets until I hit the jackpot, finding an old bottle of the most hard-core drug around in my parents' bathroom. (We'd all seen a video at school the week before called *The Road to Heroin*, after which all the football boys started talking about "scoring Oxy.") But when I'd shown up at Joni's, hoping like a complete loser to be invited into the popular girls' party, only Joni's mom had been there.

"I'm sorry, dear," she'd said. "Joni and her friends are roller-skating."

I ran home, avoided the kitchen (where Suzette was unloading groceries), dropped my bag in my room, and ran a scalding hot bath, immersing myself in the water and sobbing with my hand over my mouth for like an hour. I was never making it into the popular girls' group. I knew they were laughing at me, wherever they really were, even Jenni.

When I got out of the tub, Suzette was in my room. She looked so shocked, holding my backpack in one hand, the pills in the other. "Why, honey?" she said. "Why?"

I almost told her everything. But she was the only one left I could hurt. I shrugged and rolled my eyes. I saw her flinch as if I had punched her. Good.

Suzette had always watched me like whatever I was doing was incredible. She treated me as if I was fragile, like someone was going to grab me at any moment. Once, I wandered off in the Whole Foods and she absolutely freaked out. She had three security guards combing the store and the Houston Police Department on the way by the time she found me staring at the sugar cereals (not allowed by Suzette, of course, Wheaties all the way).

"You're safe!" she'd said, basically shouting. She'd grabbed me so tight I couldn't breathe and kept on going "You're safe! Thank God, she's right here. She's right here!" Even the cops had looked embarrassed for her, like, OK, lady, it's not like she's primo kidnapping material.

Suzette was strict about being happy the way other people are strict about bedtimes. If I mentioned feeling awkward or lonely, her face would morph into this cheerful rictus and she'd be like, "But really, everything's fine, right? Right?" If everything wasn't *fine*, it was as if I became inaudible.

Suzette made it home for dinner every single night. (This was part of her happiness regimen: hover around your daughter while in public—check; cozy family dinner—check; outsource dealing with your daughter's troubling emotions—check!)

I tried to tell her a few times about the hole, and she was there, looking right at me, but when I finished talking, usually in tears, she would say, "Now *what* should we plant in the window boxes?" or "I thought it was going to rain today but look, it's gorgeous out!" I got the message—keep it inside; brighten up, buttercup; *ferme la bouche.*

She was scared I'd turn out crazy, like her mom. She found me a therapist to talk to, grilling Dr. Sue about whether or not I showed signs of mental illness. But I wasn't crazy. I was sad. I just wanted her to listen.

On weekends, our family time was spent at the Rothko Chapel. It was like our church, but instead of believing in God, we believed in watching the way the light fell inside the chapel at various times of day. My dad's parents and sister, my namesake, Eloise, were killed in a car wreck when he was eleven. At their funeral, he told me, he realized there was no God. The priest went on and on about God calling my dad's family home, and he just thought this was bullshit.

"If there's no God," I asked him, "aren't you lonely?"

"Of course I'm lonely," said my dad.

He's like this—realistic. He doesn't butter the biscuit or whatever the expression is. "But now I have you and your mom," he said that day. "So, I don't know, maybe someone didn't forget about me after all."

What the hell? I mean, seriously! The whole conversation left me kind of dizzy. And then there's Suzette, who thinks—honestly—that she sort of *is* God. I mean, she fixes people's hearts. That's pretty insane. I just wish she knew how to fix mine.

I tried to ask Suzette about my real mom. She was a wonderful woman, said Suzette—she gave you to us. Neither Suzette nor my dad had any idea what happened to her after she handed me over. Besides, my dad hissed, hoping not to be overheard, your real mother is *Suzette*. She loves you more than *anything*.

Fast-forward to the summer of 2016, a girl underneath New York City, whizzing through a tunnel that will lead her to . . . who knows? And for that matter, who cares? The only sure thing was that it felt good to be moving.

7

Hyland

The day before Eloise went missing, Hyland finished *Happy Guy at the Wedding Smoking a Cigar*, a vaguely Rothkoesque canvas for his summer show. (Hyland kept a Rothko quote taped up in his studio: "If you are only moved by color relationships, you are missing the point. I am interested in expressing the big emotions—tragedy, ecstasy, doom.")

The title of the painting came from their friend Meg's proclamation that men underwent a torturous middle-age transformation from anxious guys who wished they were nineteen again to happy guys who smoked cigars at weddings and seemed pleased with their lives.

"They're not happy," Meg's husband, Stew, had remarked drily. "They're defeated."

Hyland disagreed with Stew, but he hadn't said so. The fact was that Hyland had a life more wonderful than he could have hoped for. Embarrassing but true: he *was* happy.

Hyland locked his studio and went for a desultory jog around the neighborhood. His knees were creaky but functional. The sun was setting by the time he returned home, their lawn an other-worldly orange in the low light. He went into the kitchen and opened a beer.

The week before, Suzette had waltzed into Ninfa's wearing a gold dress with her hair up, smelling fantastic. They'd drunk a few margaritas, wandered around the city after dinner holding hands, made out in the Uber on the way home. After the best sex they'd had in *years*, Suzette had kissed him gently and explained that she was leaving for Africa in the morning.

Goddamn Suzette! It was both a blessing and a curse to be bewitched by your wife. Without her, without Eloise, he was giddy for a few days, but then bereft. The house was so quiet.

In the shower, he used Suzette's shampoo. It had a musky, expensive scent. He pumped her age-correcting exfoliating cleanser with finely ground olive seeds into his palm, rubbed the gritty substance into his face. "Don't use my fancy products," she'd warn Eloise. "The pricey stuff is for middle-aged mothers *only*."

Oh, really, Suzette? Hyland poured a handful of awesome-smelling hair conditioner into his hand. If Suzette was going to jet off to Sudan for an undetermined amount of time, leaving her stash of aromatic potions behind, all bets were off. He was going to use her shampoo, drink their best wine, and even get ahead in "their show." A chaste rebellion, but Hyland practically cackled, thinking of how mad she would be. Maybe she'd even give him a spanking.

After his shower, Hyland slipped into his bathrobe, uncorked a great bottle of cabernet, and settled in for a *House of Cards* marathon on Netflix.

By the time Hyland waked in the morning, his head thrumming with a dull hangover, the Pringley School had called twice. One thing Hyland didn't need was news from Massachusetts. His night table held half a plate of pad thai; an unopened pack of cigarettes (he'd changed his mind by the time the Cigs4u guy arrived); an empty wine bottle; and his old, college copy of *Infinite Jest*. God, he loved that book. Funny, luminous, wise, achingly sad. He still didn't get about 90 percent of it, but that didn't keep him from drunkenly savoring his favorite sentences once in a while.

He opened the pack of cigarettes and lit a Marlboro Light right in his bed. Yup! He smoked, lay back down, felt like Brando in *Last Tango in Paris*. But without the young Parisian girl. He missed Suzette.

Hyland began to cough as his phone rang again: the Pringley School. Christ on a cracker! *I should go for a run*, thought Hyland. *As soon as I finish this cigarette, I shall go for a run*. He took the last, searing drag, stubbed out the cigarette. And then, because he was a good man who understood (though sometimes resented) his responsibilities, Hyland answered his phone.

Eloise

The Bellevue Psychiatric Hospital on Thirtieth Street is an enormous brick building. It's as grand as some of those on the Pringley campus, but it also looks sinister for sure. Off First Avenue,
there's a black iron gate, both beautiful and creepy. The whole
place seemed to me like an elegant guest arriving a hundred years
late to the ball, her gown falling into tatters.

I pushed open the gate to find an unkempt interior courtyard.
A sad tree clung to the dirt. A line of painted bricks circled a dead
bush. A tangled hose was a snake, writhing and venomous. Some
wannabe artist had covered all the ground-floor windows with
demented murals: flowers on acid, Keith Haring imitations, the
downcast profile of a black woman. And each mural was framed
by cheerful painted curtains. It was meta-weirdo, and I didn't like
it a bit.

I'd always had the assumption that Bellevue was old-school
and elegant. Sure, I knew being bipolar was no picnic, but I
thought you had to be rich and/or famous to go to Bellevue. Believe it or not, I had never even seen a picture of my crazy

grandmother—instead, I'd created an imaginary image of a regal woman, a Virginia Woolf type, brilliant and unfathomable, possessor of a mind too wild for this world. But as I stood in the most dilapidated spot I'd ever been, sorrow filled me, from my throbbing forehead down through my aching stomach.

My grandmother was just an old lady behind one of these dark windows. (Or worse, behind one of the awful paintings.)

Nothing ever turned out the way I imagined it would. I was brought up padded with secrets, when all I wanted was the truth. The stories I was spoon-fed, lovingly and with great care, didn't add up when I started examining them. Mainly the story of my real mother. But also the story of my grandmother. All anyone talked about was happy-go-lucky good times. It was bullshit!

My parents thought I needed protecting—as if I was in constant peril, on the edge of disaster. I had training wheels on my bike until I took them off *myself* at age seven. I wasn't allowed near a swimming pool without a virtual hazmat suit of sunscreen and flotation devices. Nothing in my childhood ever went wrong—from whence the panic that seeped into my days?

I was treasured, but I wasn't allowed to fuck up.

Ha! I thought. *Look at me now.*

I strode toward the door of my grandmother's mental institution, pushing the button to gain entrance. The Tape Recorder of Doom was literally screaming at me that this place was *bad, get out, run away, do not enter*, but if my early years of therapy had taught me anything, it was how to shut up the Tape Recorder of Doom.

An aside: what if the Tape Recorder is correct? This one stumped my therapist, too. Or rather, her answer was that sometimes our anxious fears *are* correct, but we can't listen to *all* of them *all* of the time. Thanks for nothing, Dr. Sue.

After I pushed the doorbell, nothing happened for a while. A few people (all men, and very dirty) walked by, seeming not to notice me. There was a guy in a wool cap sitting on the front stoop smoking. I watched him, waiting for him to look up. The door of my grandmother's mental institution opened.

"Yeah?" said a man in a flannel shirt.

"I'm here to visit my grandmother?" I said.

"This is a men's shelter," he said. "Nobody's grandmother's here."

"What?" I said. "I'm looking for Bellevue."

"This is Bellevue," he said, folding his arms in front of his chest. "But it's a homeless shelter now. They moved all the original tenants a while back."

"I don't understand," I said.

"This is not a safe place," he said. "You hear me? All kinds of people around here. All kinds. You better go, girl. Bellevue ain't got nothing for you."

I'd better go, this I understood loud and clear. But where?

9

Suzette

The news crew was waiting in the hallway again when Suzette arrived at the Heart Centre on the morning of Angel's surgery. Suzette walked past them quickly. "We wish you luck today," the anchor called.

It's not about luck, Suzette almost answered, but instead she turned back, smiled, and called, "Thank you!" without breaking her stride to Alberto's office.

Alberto's ashtray was already half-full. He seemed nervous, held out the phone receiver. "For you," he said. "Please make it short. Angel is prepped and the team is waiting."

"Hello?" said Suzette.

"It's me," said Hyland.

"Hyland! It costs a fortune to call!"

"She's missing," said Hyland, his voice sounding as if he were inside a cave.

"What?" said Suzette. She calculated the time difference: in Houston, it was midafternoon. "Who? You mean Eloise?"

"They went on a field trip to New York City," said Hyland.

"She ran away in the Museum of Natural History. Apparently, she told someone she was going to find her real mother."

Suzette sank into Alberto's metal desk chair. He lit another cigarette, raised his eyebrows.

Hyland's voice echoed on the phone line. "I'm flying up to New York," he said. "Though what I'm going to do there, I don't know."

"Wait a minute," said Suzette. "Eloise is looking for *Dorrie?* In New York?"

"Yup," said Hyland.

"How did they *lose* her?" said Suzette, anger rising in her chest.

"She said she was going to the bathroom. She turned her phone off, and then . . . who knows?"

"How long ago was this?" said Suzette.

"Sometime this morning."

Suzette put her head in her hands. "New York," said Suzette. "I took her there once, when she was six."

"I know," said Hyland.

"For her birthday."

"Yes."

Suzette could see Eloise as a six-year-old vividly, her black curls in pigtails. She'd worn a red coat with wooden toggles and matching red boots. They'd visited the Plaza, had tea and scones in the Palm Court. Eloise had wanted to ride the elevators "like the real Eloise in the books." They'd gone to a marionette show in Central Park. For a few days, Suzette had dreamed of relocating to New York, but eventually, the subways and constant fear of losing sight of Eloise wore her down. She returned to Houston with a new appreciation of her clean, dim garage with its automatic door and direct access from the car to the kitchen. In Houston, she had her own, fenced backyard with a sandbox, swing set, and no strangers.

"Jesus," said Suzette.

Alberto cleared his throat.

"I think I know where Dorrie is," said Suzette, admitting to her husband for the first time that she searched for Dorrie, once a year or so, after too much wine. "I mean, I think she might have changed her name. Taken her mother's maiden name, Black. What I'm saying..." Suzette stopped, cleared her throat, then continued. "What I'm saying is that someone named Dorothy Black lives in Hyannis, Massachusetts. It could be her. I found the name on a property record."

There was a silence that sounded like wind along the line, and then Hyland said, softly, "I know."

"You do?"

"She's a cashier at Walgreens," said Hyland.

"Really? Oh."

Hyland exhaled heavily. "I thought of Black, too. And when I had that project in Boston, I drove to the address. I followed her to work. And we were right. It's her."

"How does she..." said Suzette. "Is she...?"

"I never talked to her. She stopped at McDonald's. Remember how she'd always drink Diet Coke?"

"No," said Suzette. "I don't remember that."

"She liked sweet things in general," said Hyland. "Like tiramisu. I took her out, after the insemination. For dessert. I know it sounds kind of strange."

"I don't think it sounds strange," said Suzette. She closed her eyes and pictured Hyland, his eyes red, the way they became when he was worried. Even though she was on the other side of the world, Suzette had a small bottle of Visine in her makeup bag, in case Hyland needed it. She had a roll of strawberry Tums, for Eloise's stomachaches.

Alberto sighed, made himself known. Suzette didn't look up.

"You should call her," said Suzette. She picked up one of Alberto's pencils, stabbed herself in the thumb with its point.

"I told you, she turned off her phone." After a pause, Hyland said, "Oh, you mean Dorrie."

"Yes. In case Eloise ends up there. If we could find Dorrie on the Internet, I'm sure Eloise can."

"Eloise doesn't know her name."

"I guess not, but who knows?" said Suzette.

"Jesus Christ," said Hyland. "I don't want to call Dorrie."

"Do you want me to?" said Suzette.

"No," said Hyland. "I'll do it. And really, Suze, you should just sit tight. I can keep you posted. I can handle things on this end."

"No," said Suzette. "I'm coming home." Her stomach clenched at the thought. How had "home" become a place she was desperate to escape? How had her joyful, pigtailed daughter—with a smile that lit up Manhattan—become a sullen stranger? Suzette couldn't have tried any harder! And even now, and always, she would fly across the world to locate Eloise, to make her well.

"Please, Suzette," said Alberto, leaning across his desk. "It's time to operate."

"You don't have to come," said Hyland.

"I know," said Suzette.

"Suzette?" said Alberto, standing and moving to the door. "Let's go now, OK?"

She thought of Angel, of the news crew, of Alberto and all his hard work. But the choice was simple. "I'll be home as soon as I can," she said.

"Suzette!" said Alberto, shaking his head. "I can't do the Ross procedure, Suzette." He opened his hands, gathered them into fists. "I'll have to give Angel an artificial valve. And I'll have to tell her . . ."

"I'm sorry," said Suzette. "I am sorry, Alberto. But this is my daughter."

10

Dorrie

It was my day off and I was trying to concoct a slow-cooker dinner out of chicken thighs, some wan vegetables, and taco seasoning mix left over from Tuesday Taco Night. (Cheap boxed dinners became festive when given titles, I'd realized: Hooray, Hamburger Helper Night; Monday Mac and Cheese Celebration; Friday Night Frito Pies; et cetera.) It's been hard to afford enough food, especially since I try to keep healthy options on hand. Jayne and I clip coupons and go to Costco once a week for the basics. We mark "three-for-one" days on the kitten calendar in the kitchen. (I love cats; Jayne's allergic, so she gives me calendars and stuffed animals and mugs, even a sweatshirt embossed with a kitten. Yes, my dear one, I am a Walgreens cashier who wears a sweatshirt embossed with a kitten. As the kids say, *Deal with it.*)

We watch *Extreme Cheapskates* marathons on the Learning Channel.

Anyway, back to the story. I'd just found half a bag of egg noodles when my cellphone rang. The caller had a 713 area code.

I stared at the phone. Your father and Suzette were the only people I knew in Houston, Texas.

How could they possibly have found my unlisted cell number? I let the phone ring and ring, and then it stopped ringing. I stood in my kitchen, feeling numb. The phone chirped again—it was my boss, Marion. I answered.

"Don't even tell me he didn't show!" I said, referring to Josh, the newest hire.

"Dorrie?" said Marion, her voice sounding weird.

"Marion?" I said. "Are you OK?"

"Um, Dorrie?" said Marion. "I just got a call from the police? They need to talk to you about something. They said it's urgent."

"The police?" I said, dropping the egg noodles, which scattered all over the linoleum flooring the landlord wouldn't replace.

"They asked for your home phone, so I gave it to them. I wasn't thinking. I hope that's OK?"

"What is it?" I said, my knees buckling. "What did they want?"

"There's a missing girl in New York City. I don't understand, but they sounded pretty worried."

"OK," I said. "OK."

"If you need me to find someone to cover your shift, that's workable," said Marion, a steel-faced taskmaster who was not without empathy.

"Thanks," I said. "Yes, that would be good." I said goodbye, took a breath, and dialed the Houston number.

"Dorrie?" your father said, his voice the same. I was filled with so many emotions hearing him: my hope long since curdled to fear, my admiration for him burned into bitterness. My sorrow for how badly I had messed things up.

"Why are you calling me?" I finally managed.

"It's Eloise," said your father.

"Eloise!" I said. "You named her Eloise." I had called you Zelda for twenty months. I wonder if that name means anything to you.

"She's run away," said Hyland. "She's looking for you."

"What?" I said.

"She's having trouble," said Hyland. There was a pause, and then he said, in a very quiet voice, "She's gotten in some trouble. With drugs. We've . . . And now she's missing."

"I don't understand," I said.

"Neither do I," said Hyland. "Neither do I, Dorrie."

"Drugs?" I said. You were only sixteen! When I thought of you (as I did most days), I'd imagined you willowy and sweet, dreaming of ponies (maybe having a pony), discovering *The Secret Garden*, and peering at stars through a telescope.

"If you hear from her . . . if she contacts you . . . will you call me right away?"

"Of course," I said. "Where is she? Do you know?"

"She was last seen in New York City."

"Can I help?" I asked, three words I'd never thought I'd utter to Hyland Kendall.

"I don't know. I really don't know."

I sat down heavily. "Oh, Hyland," I said. The pain in his voice was raw. For a moment, we were both silent. Even after all this time, we were tied together. We'd created you, and now you were lost.

11

Eloise

One of the people blocking the gigantic gate between me and First Avenue freedom was a girl about my age. She wore clothes that were too big for her, jeans with a T-shirt. Her hair was kind of dirty, parted in the middle and falling lanky across her shoulders. Her skin was not great—marred by acne. What was she doing at Bellevue? The girl approached me slowly, as if she understood I was scared. "Hey, you need some help?" she said with surprising kindness. Her eyes were very blue.

I looked down, nodded. I was nervous, but also disappointed and suddenly disoriented—my whole adventure had hinged on meeting my grandmother. All the bravado that had brought me here drained away, leaving me just plain old sad. "I thought my grandmother lived here," I said, my voice embarrassingly teary and small.

"No," she replied. "No grandmothers in this place. No mothers either. Come on." She walked past the men, shoving the gate open, turning back to make sure I was following. When we'd reached the street, she said, "Where you going now?"

"The Museum of Natural History," I managed.

"Cool," she said. "I went there with my school. You see the planetarium?"

"No," I said. She was walking fast, and I tried to keep up.

"It's cool," she said.

"Aren't you supposed to be in school now?" I asked. I stammered, "I mean, isn't it a school day?"

"I don't go anymore," she said. "You?"

"I'm not from here," I said.

She snorted. "Shocker," she said.

"How could you tell?"

"Ha!" said the girl. "The *shoes*, maybe?"

I looked down. My J.Crew leopard-print ballet flats—so fashion-forward at Pringley—did look pretty stupid in the city.

"These are Jordans," said the girl, lifting a foot. "They used to be my brother's."

I nodded.

"Yeah," she said. "This was his shirt, too."

"And his pants?"

"Girl! What are you talking about? These are my damn pants!"

"Sorry."

"It's OK," she said. "Actually, yeah. They were his pants." The way she said *were* made me think he had died, rather than grown bigger. I almost asked, but for once I heeded my therapist's advice to let sleeping dogs lie, a.k.a. don't invite misery into your life unless you're prepared to process it. Or unpack it. (Dr. Sue used a lot of ambiguous verbs.)

"Thanks for helping me," I said.

"It's nothing," said the girl. "You looked like you'd seen a ghost or something."

"What were you doing there? At Bellevue?"

"My dad goes there sometimes. But he wasn't there today. I haven't seen him in a while." We reached a bus stop. "OK," she said. "You can get the crosstown bus here. Then you take the C train to Eighty-first Street." She peered at me. "Or maybe you want a taxi," she said.

I didn't want to be alone again. "Can I . . . do you want lunch or something?" I said.

"Are you paying?"

"Yeah," I said. "Sure."

She shrugged. "Why not?" she said. "Hey, let's get Indian."

"I love Indian," I said. She led the way, stopping in an unassuming deli to grab two large beers, which we were able to buy (!!) and bring to lunch, like we were adults. I hit an ATM, withdrawing as much as I could because who knew what I was going to need?

We ordered tons of cheap, fragrant dishes and that warm bread. We talked about nothing, really—movies (new James Bond, thumbs-up), music (new Taylor Swift, catchy but meaningless), clothes (she'd never heard of J.Crew; I'd never shopped on Canal Street). I went and bought two more tallboys (!!) and we finished those, too. It seemed like Fantasia (she told me this was her name, and though it clearly was not—who could really be named Fantasia?—I didn't want to argue or make her feel bad. Maybe it was her name. What do I know? Let sleeping dogs lie, et cetera) had nowhere to be. We ate and drank and laughed. After I paid the bill, Fantasia said we should go to the planetarium together. "Then you can find your teachers and deal with all that," she said.

"Yeah," I said. "Sounds good." We got two *more* tallboys (the guy at the minimart didn't even comment!), drank them on a bench, then took a taxi to the museum. Fantasia told me sheepishly that she had never been in a taxi before.

It wasn't a Journey of a Lifetime, but it was nice. We ended up buzzed, sitting in the dark, watching a false but beautiful sky. I was sorry when the show ended. I almost didn't go back to the

Pringley bus. *If she invites me to stay with her, I'll say yes,* I thought. But Fantasia just gave me an awkward handshake outside the Hayden Planetarium and said goodbye.

After Fantasia left me on Central Park West, I bought a hot dog from a vendor in front of the museum. How I was still hungry, I had no idea. The hot dog, which I covered with ketchup, mustard, *and* sauerkraut, was just so awesome. I sat down on the museum steps. There were three middle-aged ladies eating burritos near me. There were umbrella-shaded carts selling gyros, pretzels, bagels, and "paletas" (some sort of Popsicle?). Across the street, I could see tons of green trees. People in jogging clothes and women pushing strollers veered into the arboreal area. "What's that?" I asked the gaggle of burrito eaters.

"What's what?" said one of them. She was younger than Suzette, but wore an old-lady cardigan.

"That," I said, pointing to the trees.

"It's Central Park," she said, squinting at me as if I were deranged.

"Wow," I said.

"Yes," she said. She smiled with a bit of pity. I stood and decided that instead of turning myself in, I'd go for a walk in Central Park.

I really didn't have a plan at this point. I didn't have my real mother's name, and Bellevue had turned out to be a dead end. I had messed up again. I felt the hole inside me growing bigger. The Tape Recorder of Doom had been right: I *was* alone.

Suzette said I was smart, brilliant, creative. Obviously, she'd read some book about not complimenting shallow things like how your daughter looked. She read so many parenting manuals—I mean, I was like *Hello? I'm right here, and you're ignoring me to read about how to be with me!* It was absurd. And now she was in Africa.

I turned my phone on. No messages from Suzette or my dad.

But there was the name of an NYC drug dealer, the one I'd been given by a Pringley pal. I sent the drug dealer a text asking if he was near Central Park.

He responded within a few seconds that he could meet me at the zoo. He said to bring cash. I told him sure, posted an NYC selfie to lovepages, and turned my phone off again. I know, it's weird to be on the run and posting snaps to lovepages, but the few likes my picture might gather would bring me a distracted, shallow happiness, and I was looking for all the happiness I could get. Besides, when my phone was off, I was pretty sure no one could trace me. It wasn't exactly news that I was in New York City. Also, I didn't think my dad and Suzette even knew about lovepages, much less how to view my profile.

The drug dealer was waiting, as promised, by the sea lion pool. He was hot, with a dark look in his eyes that appealed to me, and blond hair in a ponytail. "You're Eloise?" he said.

"I'm Eloise."

"What can I do you for?" he said, smirking as if transposing two words counted as a witticism.

I said, "What have you got?" and he laughed, pulled out a bottle of pills.

"Let's do it together," he said.

"What is it?"

"You heard of Special K?"

"Like the K-hole?" I said. I had heard about this—again, from Fitz Hunter. When you took ketamine, a horse tranquilizer, you went down a "K-hole" in your mind where everything felt like it was OK. There were risks, Fitz had said: some people never came out of K-holes and had to be sent to an insane asylum for the rest of their lives. But otherwise, said Fitz, it was pretty fun. "You can watch your body from outside of your body" was how he put it.

"Yup," said the hot drug dealer. "Like the K-hole."

This was heavy stuff. I could hear Suzette's voice in my ear, telling me to stop this, to walk out of the park and back to the museum. "No matter what you do, you're my baby" was what she told me. But then they sent me away, like a defective toy or a puppy who couldn't be trained. I *knew* I should flee this entire situation, but I *wanted* to stay. Anticipation ebbed at the edges of my dull sadness, a neon sea on cold sand. "I don't know," I said. "Let me think about it."

He nodded, lit a cigarette for himself and one for me. We sat by the edge of the pool, watching the greasy sea lions bob around. I wanted to stay in this moment, where anything was possible for me.

12

Suzette

The flight from Khartoum to London took nine hours and fifty-five minutes. After a ginger ale and a chicken dinner, Suzette closed her eyes. She tried to send a telepathic message: *I'm coming to find you, Eloise. I'm on my way.* In a sense, this journey reminded Suzette of her insane all-night drive to New Orleans, seventeen years before. That journey, she could see now, had been misguided—but what else could she have done? Suzette rubbed her eyes, remembering again the night Patsy had brought Eloise to their door.

Eloise had been so hot, so sick. It had taken her months to recover. Suzette had taken a leave of absence from work and sat at Eloise's bedside, reading to her or just holding her hand while they watched cartoons. If Eloise woke and Suzette wasn't there, Eloise would scream in terror. What had happened to Eloise in the year and a half before she came home? Had she spent her infancy in that awful motel? Who had fed her? Had she been held, rocked to sleep? How had Dorrie allowed Eloise to become so very sick?

Suzette would never know.

But as she learned to care for Eloise—changing her diapers, listening to her babble, rushing to her when Eloise woke in the night—a slow, sad realization of how badly Suzette herself had been parented came over her like a shadow. When she was small, Suzette had had a nightmare about wolves. She'd screamed for help, for her mommy. But no one had come. In the dark, on that night and so many others, Suzette had accepted that she was alone.

But Eloise was not alone.

Carolyn had forgotten to bathe Suzette. Suzette bought her daughter bubbles and ducks and colorful washcloths, kneeling by the tub each night, rubbing sweet-smelling Eloise dry in thick towels. Carolyn had not remembered mealtimes, but Suzette rushed home every night to make it to the table, reminding Hyland to buy organic vegetables and milk. Suzette's wounds felt less raw as the years went on. As she became a mother, Suzette herself slowly healed.

The pilot's voice announcing turbulence brought Suzette back to the present. She opened her eyes, startled, realizing that she had forgotten the lesson she should have learned on the night Eloise arrived.

Suzette remembered the ride to the hospital. She had sat in the backseat, clutching Eloise as Hyland drove like a madman. Eloise had been dressed in a faded, peach-colored dress. On her feet were cheap sandals. Her hair was combed, but stuck to her hot, red cheeks. When she opened her eyes, she focused on Suzette.

Suzette's life until that moment had been structured to avoid a surprise, to ward off a miracle. But Suzette had finally stopped struggling, and Eloise had come.

In the years since, Suzette had reverted to her old ways, trying to control Eloise, trying to protect her and make her safe. And here she was again, flying across the world to manage her daughter.

If Eloise wanted to find Dorrie, Suzette realized, it wasn't Suzette's job to stop her. It was Suzette's job to give Eloise the facts and step away. Maybe Suzette could even return to Alberto and the team in Sudan. Maybe, if she let go of Eloise, Suzette could find a place for herself.

As soon as Suzette's plane touched down, she checked her messages. There was one from Meg, whom Suzette had called from Khartoum. Meg, who had fought breast cancer for three years (Suzette buying Meg ridiculous wigs at the costume shop during her chemotherapy), had recently been declared cancer-free (they'd celebrated with so many margaritas that Suzette had had to call Hyland to drive them home). While Suzette was airborne, Meg had sent five text messages. Every one read: *This is not your fault.*

Suzette waited to deplane, crushed in between exhausted, overripe passengers. It was very late at night in London. As soon as Suzette got off the plane, she bought a cup of tea, tossed back her medication. Feeling blue was one thing; feeling suicidal was quite another.

The cup with its elaborate cardboard sleeve was warm in her hands. It was hard not to think of the throngs of hungry people she'd seen in Sudan as she walked by café after gleaming café, all closed for the night.

There were hours until her connection to New York. Suzette sat alone at the gate. The lights of departing and arriving flights were small fireworks against a velvet sky. Suzette stared at her phone, desperate for a connection. She dialed her daughter.

As the phone rang, Suzette tried to figure out what to say, what message to leave for Eloise. But then, to her surprise, Eloise answered.

13

Eloise

The drug dealer and I had been sipping from his flask for a few hours, sitting close to each other, when my phone rang. The side of his leg was warm against the side of my leg. I picked up my phone and saw that it was Suzette, calling all the way from Africa to yell at me. I don't know why, but I accepted her call. I took a big gulp from the flask. "Oh, hi, Suzette," I said.

"Eloise!" she said. "Oh, honey, I'm so glad you answered. Where are you?"

"I'm in New York," I said. "Manhattan. Central Park, to be exact." There was a pause. I could practically hear her brain ticking, figuring out what to say. "Where are *you*?" I said.

"I'm halfway to you, El. I'm coming home."

"What about your big operation?" I said, failing to keep the bitterness from my voice.

"Oh, honey. You're more important. You're more important than anything."

At these words, something in me eased. I was so tired.

"Are you OK?" said Suzette. "Eloise, are you OK?"

"I'm not OK," I said. My voice was really quiet. "I'm really not OK at all," I said.

"I'll be there in a few hours," said Suzette.

"Who's my real mom?" I said.

"Oh, honey," said Suzette.

"How come I never feel OK?" I said.

"Are you . . . have you been drinking, Eloise? Have you been taking pills?"

"Please don't," I said. "Just please don't."

"OK," said Suzette. "How can I help? Sweetie, just tell me what to do."

"I don't know. I'm just so tired of feeling this way."

"It's going to be OK," said Suzette. "I'm here."

"But you're not here," I said.

"I'll be there soon, baby," said Suzette. "I'll be there so soon."

"Who's my real mother?" I said. "Just tell me!"

There was complete silence on the line. It was a moment that felt like an eternity. Suzette's breathing seemed shuddery.

"Who is my mother?" I said.

"Me," said Suzette. "I am your mother."

"Who is my mother?" I repeated.

She was quiet, and then she spoke. "Your biological mother's name is Dorrie Muscarello," said Suzette. "She changed her name to Dorothy Black. She lives in Hyannis, Massachusetts."

"Oh my God," I said.

"I love you, baby," said Suzette. "I hope . . ."

"You hope *what*?" I said.

"I hope you find what you need," said Suzette. I had never heard her sound scared, but her voice was small and terrified. I hung up on her.

"What is it?" said the hot drug dealer.

When I didn't answer, he looked at me in a way that I realized he thought was sexy. My stomach twisted. He kissed my neck.

"My name is Cory, by the way," he said. "What's yours?" His lips were cold.

I shoved him away. "Do you have a car?" I said.

"You got money, I got a car," said Cory.

I sat up, reached into my jacket for my wallet, and handed him a hundred dollars.

"Where are we going?" said Cory.

"We're going to Hyannis, Massachusetts," I said. I punched my real mother's name—Dorrie Black—and "Hyannis, Massachusetts" into an Internet search, but her number was unlisted. "Damn," I muttered.

"What?" said Cory.

"I'm trying to find an address, but it's unlisted," I said.

He snorted, the sound a rebuke. "Give it here," he said. "Who're you looking for?"

"Dorrie Black," I said, repeating the name Suzette had given me.

Within a minute or two, using God knows what illegal resources, Cory read off a street address.

"Can you take me there?" I asked. My head was pounding from the contents of Cory's flask, but my heart felt light. I was going to meet my real mother!

"Why not?" said Cory. "Let's do it. Let's go to Hyannis. Hyyyyyyyannis, Massachusetts." We both thought this was funny. It struck me that, as menacing as he tried to look, Cory was also a lonely teenager.

His car was in an underground garage. It took us a while to walk there. En route, I finished what was left in his flask. Cory's hand hurt my hand. I tripped and he yanked me up. He seemed exasperated, but I didn't care. When we got in the car, Cory turned on the heat. It felt nice. "You buckled?" he said, and I nodded.

Cory pulled out of the garage and onto the street, exiting the city within a half hour. As he drove on some dark highway, I fell asleep. When I opened my eyes, it was the beginning of morning.

"Well, OK," he said. "We're here."

"We're where?"

"Hyannis, Massachusetts," said Cory. "Listen, Eloise? I don't think you should drink any more."

"Is this happening?" I said. "It feels like all this is made up, like a stage set. You know what I mean?"

"Jesus," he said.

I didn't say anything.

"There's the house, anyway. The address? Where you wanted to go? In Hyannis, Massachusetts? We're here."

I sat up. We were parked in front of a trailer, like the ones I'd seen when my dad had once taken a wrong turn and we'd gotten lost in a bad part of Houston. A light was on in what looked like the kitchen. A woman in a fleece bathrobe was reading a book and drinking a mug of coffee. She was kind of chubby and had gray-ish, curly hair. I stared at the woman, who seemed completely engrossed in the story. She looked like me. Did she look like me?

As I watched, a teenager with tattoos entered the kitchen. He was rubbing his eyes, wearing no shirt and a pair of low-slung jeans. I could see the top of his boxer shorts. He hugged the older woman from behind, and the woman lifted her face. I held my breath. Another person—a blond woman with her hair in two braids—appeared with a frying pan full of what looked like scrambled eggs.

The boy with the tattoos walked to the window. He stood, stretching, and looked out. Could he see me? It didn't seem like it.

"Can I ask what the hell we're doing here?" said Cory. He sounded kind of nervous.

"No," I whispered. I watched the trio eat, the whole scene made warm by the overhead light. Something inside me felt warm, too.

14

Dorrie

In order to go any further in the story, I guess I have to go back. You deserve the truth, even though it casts me in a bad light. Please remember, as you read this (if you ever read this), that I was so young—only five years older than you are now. Please know that I did the best I could. Please forgive me, Eloise.

We had spent the months of my pregnancy talking about what we would do after your birth—where we could live and how. It was going to be very hard to stay in the town where we'd been hiding. There were no job prospects for me, and Jayne needed to go to school. She said she wanted a new beginning somewhere where it snowed. It's amazing to me that Jayne was twelve and yet I treated her as an equal. In fact, she seemed more mature than I. Taking care of her mother had made her both wise and immune to ordinary sadness. The challenges of begging for money and scrounging for food were no match for her. At night, she would put her ear to my belly, hoping for a kick. So we had a plan, of sorts: we would drive east (I wanted the sea) and north (snow for Jayne—she had never even seen it, hard to imagine now!) until we found a place where we could stay.

I've said it, but it bears repeating: I wanted you, and still want you, so very much, Eloise. Missing you has been my worst pain. I actually tried to find a way to describe the pain right here . . . but there are no words. And what's important isn't my hardships— it's that I love you. And hope you'll let me into your heart, just a bit, just a tiny bit, someday.

I'm sorry to say that I didn't care about Hyland and Suzette. I was sure they would keep tailing me for the rest of my life, and I knew we could elude them. As long as I never went to Texas, they couldn't take you from me.

But then you were born. I held you in my arms. And when the pains began again, both Jayne and I thought it was what the book called "afterbirth." The pain rose up, worse (it seemed) than before. And when it was over, Jayne held another baby in her arms.

This was your twin brother. His name is Zane.

15

Eloise

Cory and I sat by the beach. We had bagels with cream cheese and a small bottle of orange juice to share. I found I was ravenous. I ate my bagel quickly.

"Are you going to tell me what we're doing here in Hyannis, Eloise?" said Cory. "You just like the beach?" he said.

It was a beautiful stretch of sand, more vast and clean than any I'd seen in Texas. But I wasn't thinking about the ocean. I was still feeling weird about seeing my real mother, if that lady in the fleece robe was my mother. I'd been too freaked to get out of the car, to go to her. She hadn't wanted me, after all. When would I accept that?

Cory shook his head. "Come here, Eloise," he said. I don't know why, but I obeyed. I let him put his arms around me. He kissed me, but it was too hard. I pushed him away. "Relax, Eloise," he said, "relax." He kissed me again.

"Jesus!" I cried. "Stop it!" I said, *"Stop!"*

Cory stopped kissing me. His eyes narrowed. "You're nuts," he said. "You're fucking loony tunes, girl."

"Just give me the pills," I said. "OK? Give me the Special K."

Cory exhaled, shaking his head. "No way," he said.

"Why not?" I yelled. "Give me the pills!" The need in my voice scared me.

"Listen," said Cory. He swallowed and looked down. When he met my eyes again, he looked younger, and scared. "I stole the pills from my dad, OK? He's a vet. A veterinarian, not a Vietnam vet. Not a Gulf War veteran. He gives these pills to animals, OK? I think we should just go back to the city."

"I can't go back," I said. "I can't ever go back." I realized as I spoke that this was true. If I contacted my mother or father, I'd be sent somewhere a lot worse than Pringley. I started crying.

He shook his head slowly. "You've got issues," he said.

"I know," I said, lying back down and staring at the cloudy sky. "That really is true," I said. A lot of weird and painful emotions were bubbling in my blood, and it was like a bunch of glass shards were poking me from inside. Was my mother the lady in the fleece robe? And who were the others, the boy and the lady with the braids? Instead of feeling better, now that I was here, I felt worse. I simply wanted to feel less, to feel nothing. "I guess I just want the pills," I said.

"Eat your bagel," said Cory. "Let's just stay here awhile, watch the waves. You want to go back to that trailer park?"

"That was my mother," I said.

"Who? The lady in the trailer?"

I nodded glumly.

"Wow," said Cory. "This is a fucking trip, I'll tell you that."

"I need to be alone," I said.

Cory rose. "You know what? Fine. I'm trying to be here for you, but to tell you the truth this is way too fucked up."

"Can you leave me the pills?" I asked.

He shook his head slowly. "You're going to kill yourself," he said. "I don't want anything to do with that."

I reached into my jacket, got my wallet, and handed it to him. He opened it.

"There's three hundred dollars here," he said.

"Take it," I said. "Just give me the pills."

He made a dismissive, angry sound. He stood up and went to his car. I was crying, staring at the waves. I'd lost whatever energy had gotten me here. When I'd seen those three people in their kitchen I'd felt like . . . I'd felt like I wanted to walk in. I wanted to have some scrambled eggs with them. Ha! I was a disaster.

Cory tossed my empty wallet and a paper bag to me, started his car, and drove away.

I picked up the bag, shook it. The rattling of the pills made my stomach ease.

16

Dorrie

For almost two years, we stayed in Louisiana and cared for you both. I took my mother's maiden name. Nobody slept much. It was very, very difficult but it was possible. It's a blur to me now: the feedings, the swaddling, the crying, and . . . moments of absolute beauty, staring at your sleeping face. In our dilapidated but hidden house, you learned to crawl and then to walk. You began to babble, saying nonsense words. Your brother said, "Mama," pointing to me, but you never said the word. You hugged me, though, ran to me with your uneven gait and collapsed against me, encircling me in your pudgy arms.

And then, one sunny and mild day, you stopped wanting to eat. You got a fever; it climbed to 100 degrees, then 102. Tylenol and ibuprofen did nothing to bring your temperature down. You remained terrifyingly still, opening your eyes once in a while and looking at me blankly.

Your brother would not leave your side. He lay next to you on the mattress you shared, touching your face. If I tried to pick him up, he howled until I let him go, then crawled back to you again.

We went to the library, and I stayed with you and your brother while Jayne ran inside and typed your symptoms into the library computer: the fever, the rash, the way you shuddered once in a while, as if you were having a seizure. Your brother cried, but you were silent. Jayne returned from the library and told me we had to go to the hospital. If you weren't brought to a hospital, you could die. But if we took you in, the Kendalls would find us. I knew they would take both babies away.

I fed your brother. I tried to feed you, but you would not eat.

Jayne remained calm. She was quiet, and then presented her solution. "We can bring Zelda to the Kendalls," she said. "We can bring Zelda to the Kendalls, and they'll make sure she gets well. They'll never know about Zane. We'll be free."

Your stare was unnerving. You hadn't eaten in more than a day. In a panic, sobbing hysterically, I agreed. You seemed to grow hotter and hotter. Straight from the library, we drove.

You never know when you will be forced to make the decision that will define your days. I like to think I acted in your best interests. At times, I've even thought I was the selfless one, taking on a daily sadness in exchange for your safety. As the years have gone by, and my need for you has only grown stronger, I keep reminding myself that the Kendalls are caring for you, giving you every opportunity money can buy.

The drive felt like it was over in minutes. Before it was dawn, we were back in Texas, the state where you no longer belonged to me, at least not in the eyes of the law. I parked on K½ Street in Galveston. I gathered you in my arms. The most beautiful girl in the world. I carried you up the front walkway, over the stones where I'd drawn with chalk, up to the door I'd helped to paint. I rang the bell.

My mother answered looking confused and then angry. I told her I was sorry. I told her you were very ill, that Patsy needed to bring you to the Kendalls immediately. My mother took one look at you—your face was too flushed, your eyes glassy by now—and understood. I told Patsy I was leaving, that I would be in touch. "Tell them—make them promise, please—never to look for me," I said.

"Oh, Dorrie," she said. Her face fell with a hungover sorrow, but she nodded. The sun had turned the day brilliant. I failed to say goodbye. I held you close a final time, and whispered to you. You were so hot, and so still. I gave you to my mother.

I got back into the car, and we drove east: Jayne, your brother, and me.

In my last moments with you, I told you where I would be, if you ever needed me. I would be by the sea, I said, not knowing anything more. And you must have heard me in some fundamental way, my girl. Because by the sea is where we found you, where I next held your body, after you had grown into a skinny girl, a broken girl, the one I had abandoned.

17

Eloise

I walked along the beach for a while, holding the paper bag. I thought about calling someone for help. But who?

I saw a sign for Hyannis Whale Watcher Cruises. I had no more money, but I walked over to the ticket window anyway. A video of a whale jumping out of the sea played on a loop. It was pretty incredible, I had to admit. So big—majestic. I had a credit card, so why not?

"Shouldn't you be in school?" said the lady at the ticket counter.

I looked at her without speaking, slid my credit card across. The woman squinted at the card. "You have a photo ID?" she asked. She looked supersuspicious. I opened my wallet and showed her my Pringley identification card. She looked hard at me and at the card, but then she gave me a ticket.

On the boat, I walked away from the tourists and to the very top deck. There, I could look over the water. It was raining and cold. I breathed deeply.

A voice came over the speakers as we pulled from shore. It

went on and on about the history of whaling, how the wives would be left on land for months and months, but the men risked their lives at sea. It made me think about my real mother, how she had left me, just given me to Suzette and walked away forever.

I was in *A Midsummer Night's Dream* when I was fourteen. I played Hermia, the lead. Somehow, I got it into my head that my real mother would see the story in the newspaper about the play, and would show up in the audience. On opening night, before the show, I was lying on Suzette's bed, watching TV.

Suzette was wearing her slip and earrings. She'd applied undereye concealer—two light V-shapes under her eyes. Her hair was still wet, starting to curl in the humid evening. "Maybe my real mom will come to the play," I said.

She turned to me, hurt. But I didn't care about Suzette's feelings. I just didn't care. "It's possible," I said.

"She's not coming," said Suzette. "She told us not to look for her. I'm sorry, Eloise."

"That's not true!" I said, standing up. "Take that back," I said.

"It is true," said Suzette.

"You ruin everything!" I cried. "I hate you!"

Suzette looked down. She did not respond.

When, in the play, I woke up in the woods and couldn't find Lysander, I felt like my anger at my real mother made the lines especially poignant:

Lysander! What, removed? Lysander! Lord!
What, out of hearing? Gone? No sound, no word?
Alack, where are you? Speak, an if you hear:
Speak, of all loves! I swoon almost with fear.
No? Then I well perceive you all not nigh.
Either death or you I'll find immediately.

Of course, like an idiot, I looked out over the rows of chairs. Of course, there were Hyland and Suzette, as always. (They came to every performance of every play.) But I had really expected to see, watching from the audience, somebody who looked like me.

"Ooooh!" cried a person on the other side of the whale-watching boat. She pointed, telling her companion something in a language I didn't know. I ran over and saw a whale rise up out of the ocean, then slam back down into the water. It was awe-inspiring. I guess I hadn't really understood how huge whales were. I mean, massive! The whale came up again, all the way out of the water. My jaw dropped. I was seriously overwhelmed. And then a baby whale (according to the guy on the loudspeaker) surfaced alongside its mom. They frolicked, and that's the only word that describes it. The woman who spoke another language turned to me, and we grinned. She said something enthusiastically, and I agreed with all my heart.

We didn't see any more whales, though the cruise went on for another two hours. By the time we headed back to the dock, my elation had pretty much ebbed away. I was glad to have the pills. In the cramped bathroom of the ship, I stared at myself in the mirror. I swallowed a pill, washed it down with the lemonade I'd bought at the snack bar. I looked like complete crap.

I wished that I could stay at sea. If I had been a whaler, I thought, I could avoid land forever. But then I would have to kill whales, and that would be a real downer. Also, way too difficult. Spearing one of those enormous creatures seemed both logistically impossible and ethically wrong.

I turned on my phone. It was filled with missed calls from Suzette. Ha! I took a picture of the horizon, posted it to lovepages, and threw the phone overboard. The pill wasn't doing anything.

I felt exactly the same. I dumped a few more into my hand, swallowed them with lemonade. There were two pills left in the bottle, so I took them, too. I felt nothing, nothing, nothing.

The boat slid into its slip, and passengers disembarked. When everyone but me was off the boat, I lay down underneath some seats, just thinking I wanted to take the tour again. The next thing I knew, a man in a windbreaker was next to me, his hand on my arm.

"Are you all right, Miss?" he said.

Thanks to the ketamine, I felt a hundred miles away from this question. The man pulled a cellphone from his pocket and tapped away. He seemed frightened. It was clear to me that I needed to get off the boat.

I got up. I was unsteady on my feet, but running was my specialty. I could hear the theme song to *Chariots of Fire* in my head, and I slammed down one foot and then the other, disembarking. I reached dry land and sprinted off, toward a row of restaurants. I pumped my arms. I gasped for breath. I did not stop.

"Wait!" called the man. "Come back!"

Within minutes, I couldn't hear his voice anymore. All I could hear, as I kept moving forward, was my own body working, my blood pounding in my ears.

I found myself in a warren of old buildings. I turned in to a narrow alley, kept going until I was safely out of sight. I reached a small beach, and lay down on the sand. I wasn't trying to die. I just wanted to be numb, to stop feeling, and this isn't to say I wanted to be dead. Anyway, the sand was soft.

I closed my eyes, and I could hear a song underneath the sea. It sounded like whales—I'd heard a recording once, their cries both mournful and lovely. They, like me, were missing someone. I wished that I could swim amongst them, immerse myself, just go into the waves and let myself be enveloped by water. I was still on the sand. But I was falling deep into a warmer place.

As I fell, I couldn't stop seeing him. The boy with the bare chest and the tattoos, the boy who gazed out the window of his small house, as if he was searching, too. I heard the song, it beckoned me, and I saw him.

He was exactly my age, and somehow, we had the same face.

18

Dorrie

Most nights, after I've given Zane a mug of warm vanilla milk and a back scratch, and before I settle on the couch with Jayne for our sitcoms (unless Jayne is out with her boyfriend; on those nights, I watch TV by myself), I open this diary and think of you. When Patsy died, I had her belongings sent here to Hyannis. Little did I know, Patsy must have been in touch with the Kendalls: amongst her things was a framed picture of you. You look as if you're in first grade. In the photo, beaded barrettes hold back your unruly hair. Your expression is a bit apprehensive but hopeful—it's as if you are waiting to be told you are beautiful. (You are.) It's hard to reconcile the six-year-old girl in the picture with the descriptors I've recently been given: pill popper, runaway, anguished.

Some nights I write, usually using a fine-point Sharpie. (One of the perks of working at Walgreens is unlimited access to pens of all kinds, not to mention mechanical pencils.) Some nights, I just close my eyes and try to send happy thoughts to you. This has gone on for years; it's the perfect way to end my day. I deserve to feel the pain reflection brings. And I savor the moments when I believe everything worked out for the best. The honeyed calm I feel when Zane is safely in his room is edged with melancholy. We are all home—all safe—but someone is always missing, and it is you.

Today was different. Instead of the usual trek to work—the ringing up of strangers' intimate purchases (Pregnancy tests! Twix bars! Sleeping pills! Suppositories!), the fleeting but warm conversations with Paul about his pit bull terrier and the funny photos people have sent for processing, and the bus ride home followed by dinner, tea, and writing, I spent the day searching for you.

I drove the old Mazda through the slick streets of Hyannis—my window down, searching. I imagined every awful possibility: finding you slumped, cold, in an alleyway; seeing a glimpse of you amid the drug addicts who hung out by the 7-Eleven dumpsters; being told that yes, one of the hospitals or twenty-four-hour clinics *had* admitted a sixteen-year-old girl in bad shape.

What questions would you ask, once I held you safely in my arms? Do you think I brought you to the Kendalls because I didn't want you?

I wanted you. I want you. There are so many things I need to tell you, Eloise. I realized, as I drove around Hyannis, that when I made the awful decision to give you to the Kendalls, I'd assumed you would forget about me. I thought all the pain of our separation would be mine.

Imagining you out in the cold, and so lonely, I realized I had been wrong. But I felt as if I'd been given a second chance to find you, to care for you as I should have done from the start. Rain began falling, making the roads slippery. I looked for you, Eloise, and I yearned for atonement.

19

Suzette

It began raining as Hyland and Suzette drove north to Hyannis. "Sometimes, I just don't understand you," said Hyland. He stared intently at the road, the heavy gray sky.

"Maybe we should have told her a long time ago," said Suzette.

"Except that we promised Dorrie we wouldn't," said Hyland.

"But why? Why did Dorrie insist on hiding from us? From Eloise? It doesn't make sense, Hyland. She never asked for the money. Didn't that ever occur to you?"

Hyland cut a glance at his wife. "Yes," he said. "Of *course* it occurred to me, Suzette. But I guess I figured . . . I guess I figured it was none of our business. She gave us Eloise. To be honest, I didn't really care what the hell she was thinking!"

"Just that it all worked out," said Suzette.

"Yeah," said Hyland. After a minute or two, he said, "God, we're assholes, aren't we?"

"We're not assholes," said Suzette.

He turned to her, raised an eyebrow.

"Maybe a bit," said Suzette. "Maybe a little bit."

"We sent pictures to Patsy, didn't we?" said Hyland.

Suzette nodded. "We did," she said.

"We pay for your mother's new facility, don't we?" said Hyland. "Even though it's ridiculously expensive?"

"Yes," sighed Suzette. "Even though she doesn't deserve it," she added.

"What did that book tell you about forgiveness, Suzette?"

She sighed. "It's a four-step process," she said. "Step One: Get really mad at my mom, for all the ways she let me down."

"Step Two?"

"I'm still at Step One."

Hyland smiled, and then stopped smiling. "Is she out in this?" he said, gesturing to the rain.

"I hope she's wearing the warm boots," said Suzette. She and Eloise had gone to three shops and even the mall before finding a pair of boots that Eloise liked. "Oh God," said Suzette. "What if she isn't wearing the boots? What if she's in those flimsy leopard-print flats?"

"Try her again," said Hyland. Suzette dialed, but Eloise's phone was still turned off. Suzette shook her head. She turned on the car radio, and they listened to the news in silence, then to classical music, then to rock. Finally, Suzette turned it off.

"We're almost there," said Hyland, taking the exit toward the Sagamore Bridge.

"What was it like, talking to Dorrie after all this time?" said Suzette. "What did she sound like?"

Hyland exhaled. "She was confused, I guess is how I'd put it. She seemed annoyed that I'd called, short with me. But then I told her Eloise was missing. I told her . . . about the drugs."

Suzette looked at her hands. "What did she say?"

"She was alarmed. She said she'd start looking for Eloise, and that she'd call us if she heard anything."

"Was she mad at us?"

"Mad at us? What do you mean?"

"For messing up," said Suzette.

"Oh, Suzette."

"I used to hate her," said Suzette, touching the car window. It was cold.

"And now?"

"I guess I'm still angry with her, but . . ."

"But what?"

"I guess you can never know why people do what they do. I wouldn't have been able to give Eloise away either. I live in fear of losing her."

"Really?" Hyland's tone was kind, surprised. She could tell he wasn't judging her, but felt sorry for her. He loved her, Suzette knew, and he wished she could find peace.

Suzette nodded, stared at the rain. "Sad but true," she said.

They crossed the bridge, and followed Route 6 to Barnstable and then Hyannis. Past the small downtown, they turned left. It continued to rain. They passed large homes and then smaller ones. When they saw a sign for Cinnamon Shores, Hyland turned. Dorrie's street was lined with small, neat mobile homes. "It's number sixty-two," said Hyland. They pulled into the driveway of a double-wide with white vinyl siding.

"It doesn't look like anyone's here," said Suzette.

"I should call, I guess," said Hyland. He dialed, then said, "No answer."

They sat in the car for a while, the engine on, heater running.

"What are we supposed to do now?" said Suzette.

Hyland stared at Dorrie's home. He didn't answer. Then he shrugged on his winter coat (Suzette hadn't seen it in years), and walked to Dorrie's front door. He pushed the doorbell, crossed his arms over his chest. His breath was visible in the cold air.

Suzette realized that she didn't have any warm clothes. The jeans and cotton sweater she wore would hardly get her through a day in Massachusetts. She thought of Eloise, all the outfits they'd bought, the way Eloise had surveyed herself critically in the dressing room mirror. Suzette turned off the car and ran to join Hyland. "Don't leave me alone with my thoughts," she said, burying herself in his arms.

"Look," said Hyland. He pointed through a window in the front door.

Suzette looked in. "Yeah, lots of coats," she said. "Scarves and hats. What?"

"There, in the corner."

Suzette narrowed her eyes and saw two hockey sticks and a hockey bag, underneath a New York Rangers jacket. "You mean the hockey stuff?" she asked.

"Look at the bag," said Hyland. His face was strange, his expression almost childlike, as if he'd just been handed a wrapped box containing everything he'd ever wished for.

"The bag?" said Suzette. "It looks like your hockey bag, Hyland."

"There's a name on the bag," said Hyland. He grabbed Suzette's hand. "A boy's name, there on the bag. Zane."

20

Dorrie

Jayne needed to go to work at 3:00 P.M. I was tired and worried, frantic to find you, Eloise. But as she stepped from the car in front of the condominium where she was taking care of an elderly man, Jayne turned to me. "Don't forget about Zane," she said. It was like a punch to the stomach. "You can't keep him in the dark," said Jayne. "Not anymore."

I nodded. Jayne gave me a quick hug and shut the door.

I picked up my phone and called him. "Moms!" he answered, his voice (as always) enthusiastic and loud.

"Hi, Zane," I said.

"I'm walking into b-ball practice. What's up?"

"I need to talk to you, honey," I said.

"What's the matter?"

"Nothing. Nothing, honey. But I need to speak with you. Right away."

"Okaaaay," said Zane. "Are you giving me the Mazda?"

I laughed. I'd promised Zane my old Mazda when I could afford a new car. He'd already told me he was going to use spray paint to turn the rusted dents in its body into flames. "Not a chance," I said. "But can you skip practice today? It's important."

"I don't know, Mom," said Zane.

"I'll pick you up in ten minutes."

"Can we go to Subway?"

"Sure, Zane." I hung up, smiling.

It's hard to believe how much your brother eats. It began when he was twelve, his "race to the moon," as I called it. For that birthday, he'd invited ten friends to sleep over, telling me he'd much rather a stack of rental movies and Costco pizzas than a party at Balls to the Wall or Wackenhammer's Arcade, places he knew I couldn't afford. He's thoughtful like that—and has never seemed embarrassed to bring his rich friends over. They sprawl across the Goodwill couch, eat bowls and bowls of popcorn (the cheapest snack in the world, even if you splurge on butter), and drink Rite Aid–brand cola. If I make chocolate-chip cookies, they literally stand up and cheer. Sometimes a sweaty boy hugs me.

For Zane's sixteenth birthday, Jayne and I scoured the Craigslist ads for a Nintendo, finally locating a used one in Falmouth. Zane was thrilled to find it next to his stack of birthday pancakes, and instead of complaining that the Nintendo was a decade old, he called it his "vintage gaming system," and his friends played along, pretending Pong and Frogger were just as thrilling as their fancier games.

Your father and Suzette had kept their promise to leave me alone. They didn't know about Zane, and while sometimes I thought he could use a father's input (and a father's money), I was too afraid to reveal any more than the basics to Zane: yes, he had once had a father. His father had been extremely smart and artistic; he'd taught me about the painters in all the art books I'd bought Zane at Barnes & Noble. Yes, Zane looked like his father. No, Zane couldn't meet his father, because his father was dead.

What else could I say? If I told Zane any version of the truth, he might leave me. Who wouldn't choose Suzette and Hyland and their enormous mansion? You probably had the best of everything: handmade wooden toys, smocked dresses, brand-new books with no missing pages or crayon scribbles in the margins. Beautiful shoes.

So I fibbed. A tragic fishing trip accident, I told Zane: no survivors. When he asked for a rod and reel, I bought it (my heart sinking at his sweet attempts to commune with a mirage). When he hung around the harbor, even getting a summer job at the dock, I said nothing, rising at dawn to drop him off, rinsing out his bait buckets and Goodwill galoshes. I bit my lip when he began to get tattoos of oceanic disaster scenes: towering waves, rising ships, dark skies.

And now, on a rainy Wednesday afternoon, I was going to have to tell him the truth.

There is no good way to tell your son you are a liar. I was prepared for Zane to be furious, appalled. I was assuming he would stand up and walk out of Subway. I thought he'd cry. Instead, your brother listened and continued eating his Meatball Marinara sandwich as I told him everything: the agreement I'd made with your father and Suzette; the way I'd run to New Orleans; the night I gave you to the Kendalls and drove away with him. Zane knew the rest. We'd ended up in Hyannis, where he'd grown up doted on by a teenager and a youngish single mother. We hadn't been able to afford tennis lessons, sailing camp, or fancy running shoes. He'd worn used clothes. We loved him.

I finished the story. Zane finished chewing, wiped red sauce from his lips with a napkin. "So my dad's alive?" he said.

I nodded.

"Can I meet him?" asked Zane.

I nodded again, a sour taste in my mouth. Zane took my hand. "Mom, what?" he said.

It was hard to put into words. I was embarrassed. I told him I was afraid he'd choose your father over me. I didn't want him to leave me.

"Oh, Moms," said Zane. He squeezed my hand and let it go. "I belong to you, come on," he said.

I'd raised him. I should have known.

When Zane had finished eating, I told him you were missing. "Apparently, she's looking for me," I said.

"What's her name again?" said Zane, pulling out his iPhone (barely paid for every month, but I made do).

"Eloise. Eloise Kendall," I said.

He pecked away for a few minutes. I sipped my coffee. Then he said, "Yeah, she's on lovepages. Everybody is."

"I'm not," I said.

"I mean everybody *young*," said Zane. "No offense, Mom."

"None taken," I said. He peered at his phone. "People post pictures and whatever," he said. "Oh, fuck. I mean oh, no. Look, Mom."

He handed me the phone. On the screen was a blurry photograph of the ocean. "I don't understand," I said.

"Look in the distance," said Zane, using his fingers to enlarge the photo. "That's Millway Marina. She's here. She's by the water."

"Oh, honey," I said. We stood, Zane packing up the last of his sandwich to eat in the car, and we ran across the lot. In minutes, we reached the marina. I parked, and Zane leapt out. "Now what?" I said. "Now what?"

"I'll find her," said Zane, taking off. I stood by the car, shivering, watching him run, my strong boy in his neon shorts and a cheap windbreaker.

"Go ask at the ticket desk!" called Zane. "She must have taken that picture from out on a boat!"

I sprinted toward the Whale Watcher Cruises desk, dropping

my coffee cup on the ground. But when I reached the ticket window, I found it was shuttered for the day. The last cruise had ended at four. "Eloise!" I cried, hoping you could hear me, hoping you could sense me. I began to jog along the water. I knew you were near. I knew you were in trouble. And then I heard a voice call out.

"Mommy!"

For a minute, I thought it was you.

"Mommy!"

But the voice was Zane.

"Mommy!" he cried, and I followed the sound. Down an alley by the boardwalk, I found my son. He was kneeling on the ground, holding a teenage girl in his arms. The girl was thin, deathly pale, her long curly hair the same shade as Zane's. The thought came to me unbidden: *They could be twins.*

"Mommy," said Zane, "I found her."

21

Hyland

Sometime in the night, Hyland stood up, needing escape from the hospital room, if only for a few minutes. "I'm going to go find some food," he said. "Want anything?"

Suzette shook her head. She held one of Eloise's hands. Eloise breathed in and out, her eyes closed. Was she going to die? Hyland couldn't bear it. He simply could not. He walked toward the doorway and exited.

As he had hoped, the boy was there. He looked so much like Hyland as a teenager that it was a shock. The most wonderful shock in the world. He looked up from his video game when Hyland approached. Dorrie was asleep with her head on his shoulder. "Sir," he said, stiffening.

"You don't have to call me *sir*," said Hyland.

The boy smiled nervously. "What should I call you, then?" he asked.

Hyland almost said it: *Dad.* But he was not the boy's father any more than Dorrie was Eloise's mother. "How about Hyland?" he said.

"OK," said the boy. "How is . . ." he said. He swallowed, then said, "How is my sister?"

"The same."

"I didn't even know I had a sister. I didn't know, until today." He paused. "But maybe I did kind of know. Somehow, I did kind of know."

Hyland thought of many things to say, but none of them were kind to Dorrie. He nodded.

"Maybe I could . . . maybe when this is over . . ." said the boy.

Hyland fought the urge to grab the boy, to hold on to him. "Maybe you could come visit us," said Hyland. "I hope you will."

"That would be awesome," said the boy. Quietly, he said, "I didn't know I had . . . I didn't know about you either, sir. Hyland, I mean."

"I'm so sorry about that," said Hyland.

"Yeah."

"But we know now," said Hyland. The boy grinned. They looked at each other for a moment. "You play hockey?" said Hyland.

"Yes, and soccer. And basketball," said the boy.

"I played hockey, too."

"Oh yeah?"

"Yeah."

Words failed them both. The hallway was bright. The boy looked back at his game. Hyland put his hand on the boy's shoulder. A boy who played hockey, a son. And for Eloise, if she made it, *when* she made it, a brother.

22

Suzette

Who is her mother?

When Suzette was alone with Eloise, as the hours passed and she did not wake, the nurse's question seemed to hang in the air. Suzette had been a frightened child. With the strength of her own will, she had made herself into a doctor and a wife. But another force had changed her when Eloise arrived. It had felt like being burned, being hammered, slowly finding the right shape. Being forged into a mother, a good one or bad—and maybe she was both—was the hardest thing Suzette had ever done. Or more precisely, the hardest thing that had ever been done *to her.* It was still so hard.

There wasn't any answer, at least not one Suzette could understand. But the metaphor of remaining still next to Eloise, of contemplating the worst possibilities but not fleeing, this seemed a start. The mother is the one who sits and waits. And even as her heart cries out for her to save herself, to run, she does not.

The mother is the one who stays in the room.

23

Eloise

My mom told me once about how a baby's heart forms, like origami in the womb. Certain cells are programmed to be the cells of the heart; they form a long tube that pumps the blood. Then somehow, this tube just knows how to turn and loop itself, fusing into a tiny, perfect organ. "Isn't it just amazing that it *works?*" Mom used to say, shaking her head in wonder.

This is what it felt like as I found my way to consciousness after my overdose—a twisting and turning, looping through what seemed like a dark tunnel. I felt as if someone at the end of the tunnel was guiding me, showing me how to rise up above a darkness that was both beckoning and final.

I opened my eyes. I was in some sort of hospital room. It was dim and blurry. A figure came into focus slowly, its edges becoming clear, then the fact that it was a person. Her expression was soft, her red hair loose.

It felt like an impossible dream. I had come so far, tried to hurt her in every way, kicked so hard, lit fire to every bridge.

"Mom?" I said. "Is that you?"

She leaned toward me. And though I was probably on morphine, and maybe that was why I felt the hole inside me grow a little smaller, I suddenly understood that if I just kept looking at her, I might be able to find a way back home.

She smiled. She put her hands—they were warm—around my face.

"Mom?" I said.

And Suzette said, "Yes."

Acknowledgments

Thanks and love to my family of friends in Austin, Texas, and Ouray, Colorado: Clay Smith, Paula Disbrowe, Caroline Wilson, Moyara Pharis, Mary Helen Specht, Dalia Azim, Kathy Blackwell, Owen Egerton, Doug Dorst, Mary Maltbie, Cory Ryan, Erin Kinard, Alexia Rodriguez, Pam Parma, Bridget Brady, Tina Donahoo, Stacey Gardner, Rachel Wright, Jaye Joseph, Jenny Hart, Ben Tisdel, Ben Fountain, Dominic Smith, and Emily Hovland.

Dr. Hanoch Patt was kind enough to answer all my questions about the heart, and he is a treasured friend and pancake date, as well. Thank you, Hanoch.

I am so grateful to the team at 1745 Broadway, especially Gina Centrello, Jennifer Hershey, Kara Cesare (whose conception of this novel as a triangle missing one side was astonishing and so helpful), Cindy Murray, Benjamin Dreyer, Emma Caruso, and Kim Hovey.

• • •

As always, thank you to my extended family: the Meckels, the Toans, the Westleys, the Bennigsons, and the McKays.

Thank you, F. E. Toan, for listening when I told you I was stuck, and for giving me the words of wisdom that helped me to finish this novel.

Michelle Tessler, my agent and friend, helped me talk through this book as we hiked the Blue Lakes Trail in Colorado. Michelle, I'm looking forward to another fifteen years of conversations about love, mountains, and books with you.

My heart is for my family: WAM, THM, and NRM. Your crazy love makes my life a joy.

I remember when I first saw Tip Meckel's smile at a party in Missoula, Montana. He lit up the room and continues to be the light of my life.

About the Author

AMANDA EYRE WARD is the critically acclaimed author of six novels, including *How to Be Lost, Close Your Eyes,* and *The Same Sky*. She lives in Austin, Texas, with her family.

amandaward.com
@amandaeyreward
Find Amanda Eyre Ward on Facebook

About the Type

This book was set in a Monotype face called Bell. The Englishman John Bell (1745–1831) was responsible for the original cutting of this design. The vocations of Bell were many—bookseller, printer, publisher, typefounder, and journalist, among others. His types were considerably influenced by the delicacy and beauty of the French copperplate engravers. Monotype Bell might also be classified as a delicate and refined rendering of Scotch Roman.